Trusting my Billionaire Boss

By:

LEENA D'WYNTER

Contents

Chapter 1

Lacy

MY FAKE NAME WAS now real.

I rubbed the glossy letters next to my passport photo, boldly declaring Lacy Armstrong was the name of the slightly apprehensive woman in the picture. It was probably the facial expression I always wore in new situations. And everything was new right now.

I tucked the passport into my purse, then resumed packing. I had finally managed to win the five-day cruise my company offered every year to its most impressive employees. I could have won it earlier, but my fake name hadn't been real yet. The stupid courts kept finding my reasoning insufficient, but my perseverance proved fruitful and I was free from the chains of my past at last.

My phone buzzed. A text from my roommate—the only one who knew of my hidden past.

I have to talk to you right now. Please say you haven't left for the airport yet!

I have about an hour, I texted back. *What's up?*

Be there in twenty.

She arrived in sixteen minutes. The look of horror on her face as she barged into our small studio of an apartment made me abandon my packing at once.

"Sarah, what's wrong?" I asked as she marched to the couch. It was the first thing I had bought with legally earned money from my current job, the one Sarah had helped me get.

My roommate sat rigidly on the couch, her black hair hanging like a curtain across her face. Her body language—head bowed, shoulders hunched, and hands balled into tight fists—screamed fear. I hadn't seen her like this in years, not since her brother finally got himself in enough trouble to land in jail for nearly a decade.

"I have a question," she began, her voice tight as if struggling to keep it even, "and I need an honest answer."

I sat opposite her, apprehension building. "You know I'm always honest with you."

She took a long, labored breath. "If I confess I've stolen a million dollars, would you help me?"

The blood drained from my face, grabbed my stomach on its way down, and hid at the bottom of my shoes. I had known Sarah for five years and I would've sworn in every court that she would never do such a thing. But she had an autoimmune disease and the medicine wasn't cheap. And she had her messed-up brother, who seemed determined to dig an early grave.

My first instinct was to assure her I would do everything in my power to keep her safe. We were all the family each other had and we'd sworn to be there for each other no matter what. But fury ballooned through my entire being at the thought. I did not want to live this life again! I just got my new name. My new lease on life! I loved Sarah as a sister, but I couldn't throw away the last seven years of pulling myself out.

And yet, Sarah couldn't survive on her own. Not with that autoimmune disease of hers. She'd literally die if I abandoned her.

I opened my mouth, but everything inside me screamed against helping her. I couldn't do this again. Not even to save Sarah's life. I was the worst person on the planet, but I couldn't live another life filled with fear, managing thousands of lies and praying no one looked too closely at me.

I took a shaky breath. "No."

Sarah hunched over, covering her face with her hands.

I reached out to her. "I am so sorry—"

She dropped her hands and stared at me, her face full of relief. "I am so glad you said that!"

I dropped my hand. "What?"

"I haven't stolen anything. I needed to know if you would be the type that would help me abscond with a million dollars."

I sputtered for a good minute. Fury, relief, and confusion warred inside me, all fighting to come out at once.

"Why would you do that?" I finally demanded. "You know how hard I've worked to escape that life! Why would you think I would be stupid enough to return to it?"

"I'm sorry, Lacy! I freaked out and I didn't know if your father had somehow sucked you back into that world."

The mention of my father made me want to gag. He was the reason I ended up in jail at the age of sixteen. Granted, he had also gone to jail, but he had failed to teach me anything about how to not end back up in there.

"You know I have no contact with my dad, and even if I did, I would never steal again."

"I know, but it makes sense that they would think you did."

My poor emotions went through another whiplash. "*Who* thinks I did what?"

She grabbed my cold hands. "I don't know the details. I just happened to be at the right place at the right time, and I overheard Kevin on the phone. Someone's been skimming the account for months, totaling up to about three million. And"—she squeezed my hands—"they think *you* did it."

My stomach dropped into my shoes again. They must have found out about my dad. I knew enough from my dad's world of lies that I had not fabricated my new life very well. But I hadn't wanted to fill my new life with so many lies that it wouldn't look any different from the life I had left behind. I had hoped that if I kept my head down, didn't make any waves, and worked hard, no one would realize the quiet, hard-working girl was once embroiled in mass swindling.

But now someone was skimming the accounts I worked on. Kevin, my boss, must have noticed the discrepancy when he'd been promoted last month. He had taken over once our old boss had retired and I had learned real quick—in a panic—that he had extreme attention to detail. It wouldn't have taken him long, once he discovered the skimming, to do a deep dive into the lives of all his employees in his department. And all my lies, told for a chance at a new life, had led me straight into a trap instead.

Of course they'd blame me. I had a prison record and they needed a head to roll. I've seen others like me get innocently tossed in jail for less. No jury was going to believe I was innocent. Not with my past.

"So much for going on that cruise," I muttered, the pain and anger forming a knot in my chest. It would have been the first vacation I had taken in years, the first time I'd ever stepped on a boat. But the dream was gone. Up in smoke because of my stupid web of lies.

"No!" Sarah cried. "You should definitely go! It might be the only thing that saves you!"

I stared at her. "Please don't tell me you're suggesting that I should run and disappear on one of those islands." It would be another life full of lies.

She shook her head. "I'm not saying you should make a run for it. I'm saying that your boss's boss and his boss and who knows how many other bosses are going to be there, including David Wellington!"

David was the CEO of our company and normally worked at our headquarters in New York City. Sarah had met him once when he had attended a company party here in Chicago to announce his takeover of the company from his father. I had been sick that day and since he only bothered to see important people whenever he dropped by our branch, I had failed to meet him yet.

"You'll be able to have his undivided attention!" she continued. "You could explain everything!"

"And what am I going to say? 'Hi, I lied about my name, my past, and my resume for the past five years I worked under you, but I swear, this time, I really am telling the truth and that I didn't take all that money. Please believe me?'" I snorted in bitterness. "No one is going to believe that."

"But he's a guy!"

"I fail to see how that is relevant."

"You're a girl! Sometimes guys will go easy on girls."

I glared at her. "If I'm understanding what you're implying, I vehemently disagree with it. I'm not turning on the charm to save my life." That was my dad's specialty. He scammed so many women with his seductive charm, stealing their inheritances while blowing them kisses. And I refused to turn into him.

"You don't have to flirt with him," Sarah countered. "Just explain the facts. You're very honest—I'm sure he'll believe you."

"You're forgetting an important fact."

"What?" she asked.

"The fact that not even my best friend and roommate believed I was innocent at first."

She flushed. "I'm sorry. I panicked. Kevin sounded so sure it was you and with your history—"

"And yet, you think some stuffy, rich CEO is going to believe my side after he's read the long list of how my father scammed others with his honed lying skills?"

She squeezed my hands. "Just try, okay? It can't hurt, right?"

My phone buzzed—my alarm telling me I needed to head out the door. I took a shaky breath, wanting to curl into a ball and hide somewhere. But Sarah was right. My chances were basically nonexistent; it couldn't hurt to try. And, at the very least, I could enjoy the vacation since it might very well be my last. Vacations, after all, weren't a thing in jail.

Six hours later found me standing in the long line winding up to the entrance to the cruise. I stared up at the big ship, impressed such a gigantic heap of metal didn't sink at once. I knew very little about boats, but I did know this one was stocked full of entertainment for its guests, with big suites for the super rich and tiny cabins for the not so rich. Since this trip was a gift from my company and I was on the lower end of the valuable employees—and now even lower—I assumed I would be experiencing one of the small cabins.

Honestly, I didn't care what I was assigned. I just wanted to be out on the open water, enveloped by the salty air and pretending my life wasn't about to implode.

I scanned the crowd, wondering if the CEO of my company was in line, too. Then I laughed at myself. There were two lines, and he obviously would be in the red carpet section for the VIPs. In fact, I bet he was already in his fancy suite, sipping something cold while us underlings waited in the sweltering heat.

A commotion murmured through the crowd, originating from behind me. I turned like everyone else, trying to get a glimpse as to what was going on. It soon became obvious when a sleek limo pulled up to the start of the VIP line. A man completely clad in black and, obviously, a member of a security team jumped out and opened the door for the important person he worked for. Out stepped a man dressed in an overly colorful Hawaiian shirt and dark slacks, as if he was trying to make a statement about what business casual should really mean. But it wasn't his clothes that caused my involuntarily gasp. No, it was his face and physique. That was one good-looking guy. And, judging by his grin as he swept over the adoring crowd, he knew it. He waved at us as though he was some celebrity, even blowing kisses at a few giggling women.

Revulsion crept up inside me. He was too much like my dad. I turned away and stared at the cruise ship, determined to not let him get one more ounce of attention from me.

Chapter 2

David

I RUBBED MY TEMPLES in exasperation as my friend Josh stepped out of the limo and waved at the crowd as if he was on the red carpet to the premiere of a movie he had starred in. And while I knew that was Josh's secret dream, I did not appreciate him trying to enact that dream every time I took him somewhere.

"I thought," I growled from the inside of the limo, "you promised we wouldn't be noticed this time." Unlike him, I hated being the center of attention and disliked walking up the VIP walkway with everyone staring at me, no doubt wondering why I was so important.

"I promised you wouldn't be noticed," Josh quipped. "And you won't!" He strolled away, heading up to where the VIPs checked in, waving and smiling at the crowd, who acted as if he really was a celebrity. Technically, he kind of was. He dated enough high-profile girls that he'd managed to gain his own cult following.

I grumbled for another minute, then stepped out of the limo. And then muttered again when I realized Josh was correct. Not a single person looked my way. All eyes remained on Josh as he waltzed to the check-in counter. I followed after Josh as if I were just a boring manager even though my net worth easily doubled his—a fact I liked to rub in his face whenever he got a bit too cocky.

I scanned the crowd out of habit, then stopped on a girl with wavy, light brown hair. With everyone staring at Josh, she stuck out like a sore thumb with her head turned away, her chin held high, a hand on her hip as though she had no interest in the diva charade Josh was orchestrating. Was she one of Josh's exes? Her face was in profile to me but she seemed slightly familiar. It would explain her distaste. Josh had never been big on commitment in relationships.

"It wouldn't be fair to other women" was Josh's catchphrase.

This girl was probably regretting booking the cruise—maybe even debating whether to turn around and hightail it out of here. Being stuck on a ship for five days with an unrepentant ex wouldn't be fun.

"Sir?" a cruise employee piped up from behind me.

With a jolt, I realized I had stopped, all my attention captured by that girl. I immediately resumed a fast pace and shot a look at the girl, hoping she hadn't noticed my stare. To my relief, she seemed intent on boring holes into the looming cruise ship instead of checking to see if anyone was checking her out. Not that I was checking her out. Yes, she was pretty and I rather liked her nose while in profile, but pretty women and I were not a good combo. The encounter usually ended up with me acting like some stammering fool who had failed to graduate elementary school. Which was beyond frustrating since I could command a boardroom, make hard decisions, and double my company's net worth in a year, yet I failed to string two complete sentences together when I crushed on a girl.

Enough of her. I had bigger problems to worry about. Someone had siphoned three million over the past eight months from my company. And I had yet to inform my father.

Just the imagined look of disappointment on his face made me more nervous than the presence of a pretty girl. I had fought tooth and nail to convince him to give me control over the company so he could retire early and start taking care of his health problems. The first two years went well, but it would be humiliating for me to confess that this year, I lost three million to some thief.

I was usually on top of things, constantly going over all the accounts. But the siphoning had been small, less than a hundred dollars, happening regularly several times a week. I had considered it legit. Thankfully, one of my employees—a newly promoted employee eager to make his mark—had realized it wasn't anywhere near legit.

The man also identified the thief, a Lacy Armstrong who worked under him in the accounting department. She had recently been promoted about the same time the money started to disappear and had the access to pull it off. Worse, she had a prison record for swindling.

How that had escaped the background checks, I probably would never know, but I was already putting guidelines in place to make sure it didn't happen again.

When I reached Josh, I found him frowning at me, but when he didn't voice his opinion, I finished the check-in, then followed the cruise employees as they led us to our suite.

"This is terrible!" Josh announced as he strode into the large suite with a dining area, sitting area, guest bathroom, balcony with a hot tub, and a partitioned-off bedroom. "I have to share this with you? Why didn't you arrange for me to have my own suite?"

"Cheaper." I sat down in the dining area, my back to the full-pane glass windows since they showcased the harbor and I had no desire to stare at that.

"David Wellington, I know full well you could afford to buy the whole ship if you wanted."

"This is a company retreat," I countered as I pulled out my laptop. "And you're my guest, so you may have missed the part in the rules where it fails to state that Josh Covens can have his own suite 'cause he whined loud enough."

"I get the bed, then."

"No, you get the couch."

Josh snorted. "I forgot this is why I don't go on trips with you." He stretched himself out on the long couch. "You pinch pennies as bad as your old man did."

"Thank you," I said, unrepentant.

"You better not skimp out on paying me for catching your thief for you," he griped.

I rubbed my temples, not entirely happy about the situation. Josh had been with me when I had first learned of the stolen millions. While the initial evidence pointed to Lacy, my investigators had cautioned they needed more before I could toss her into jail. My next move was to revoke the award that allowed her to join the company retreat—since she obviously didn't deserve it—but Josh insisted that might cause her to run before we could nab her. He offered a different plan: He'd join me on the cruise and use his honed womanizing skills to pump whatever incriminating evidence was needed against her.

"It will be like a sting operation!" he had said. "It will be so much fun!"

Since I had seen him work his magic many times, I had agreed on the spot, but now I wished I hadn't. My lawyers had insisted I didn't need any more evidence. She had a record already of doing something similar, she'd lied about who she was, and she had the access and motivation to pull it off. It was going to be the easiest case possible.

Still, I couldn't very well cancel bringing Josh along when he had dropped everything to come with me.

Not wanting to deal with the whole mess anymore, I refocused on my laptop. Work was the easiest way to deal with stress.

"So," Josh began, ruining my concentration, "when do I meet the babe?"

"Eight tonight," I said, refocusing on the spreadsheets before me. "We're all meeting in a reserved ballroom for initiation."

"And she has no idea?"

"I hope not." I didn't want her disappearing into the Bahamas, never to be found again. Telling my father that I had lost three million was bad enough. Informing him that the culprit slipped away while on a trip paid by the company would make that ten times worse.

"Good." Josh rubbed his hands for a second, then frowned. "Wait. You can't work in here."

That made me look up. "Why not?"

"'Cause if I bring her in here, you're going to make it awkward."

"Find somewhere else to take her, then."

"David, women love wealth, and this suite screams it. I need it to do my magic. Besides, I bet you stay in here the entire time during these company retreats, don't you?"

I hunkered down, refusing to respond.

"Nope, this will not do." Josh marched over to me and swiped for my laptop but I dodged his move.

"What are you doing?"

"You are going to actually experience a real vacation. Give me that thing."

"I have work."

"If you're going to force me to work out of my comfort zone, then I'm going to insist you do the same thing. Either you lose the laptop or you take it out of this room, but you don't get to work in here. This is now my office."

"I paid for this!"

"But I'm more annoying," Josh shot back with an evil grin. I knew that look. It was the one he wore when he was willing to lose everything before he budged from his position. I'd seen him throw it at teachers during our days in boarding school and while he may have lost a few times, he always made sure the other side lost more.

"Fine." I grabbed my laptop, shoved it into my bag, then stormed out. "But if you're late for the meeting tonight, I'm consigning you to sleeping on the floor."

Josh gasped as if I had threatened to toss him overboard, but I knew his horror was fake. I muttered darkly as I strode toward the elevator, then hastily forced on a polite smile when a couple scooted around me with furtive looks. Keeping that fake smile in place, I rode the elevator to the main deck, then prowled until I found an empty chair. With relief, I settled into it and pulled out my laptop to throw myself into work again. It was the easiest way for me to relax, a trait I had inherited from my father. My sisters and mother thought we were nuts, but, as my father would say, it was cheaper than paying for therapy. Rather, it made money.

I wasn't sure when I looked up next. Maybe an hour or two; work was easy to get lost in. But I was surprised to find the aloof girl from the waiting line standing less than fifty feet from me to my left. She leaned against the railing, eyes on the ocean as though lost in her own private world. I couldn't help wondering what she thought about. By the way she hunched her shoulders, it didn't seem a very happy inner world. Yet she had seemed so calm and put together earlier.

Half of me wanted to stroll up to her like I'd seen Josh do and start a conversation. But the wise side of me knew I'd only stick my foot into my mouth and look like a fool. Best to keep my wishes to myself.

Speaking of Josh, he abruptly sat down beside me. "The world must be ending."

I eyed him. "Why?"

"You are cheating on your laptop."

"What?"

He grinned and tossed his head toward the girl against the railing. "You're eying something other than your laptop for once."

I shot out the first excuse that came to mind: "I was thinking she's probably one of your exes."

That wiped the teasing look off Josh's face and he studied the girl for a long moment, a frown growing. Then he shook his head. "I don't think so."

Now it was my turn to tease. "Not sure, are we? Can't keep all those girls straight in your head?"

Josh shrugged. "I only remember the ones I severely didn't like, and she isn't one of those. So, I'm okay with re-meeting this one. Maybe the second time will go better."

I didn't like that conclusion. "I don't think she will like that. She was not impressed with your grand entrance earlier."

"Really?" He stroked his chin, his eyes on her. "Then that means she'll be a challenge. I love challenges. This should be fun."

Josh stood up but I grabbed his arm. "Don't. Leave her alone. She seems like she is enjoying being by herself."

He shook off my arm. "Robbed of my own suite, forced to sleep on a couch, and now you're forbidding me from checking out the market? David, you're going to kill me on this trip."

I let go of him. "I'm not saying you can't. You can. Just not *her*."

A slow, evil smile spread over his lips. "You like her!"

I recoiled. "I don't even know her. We've never met."

"Oh, I can fix that!"

Before I could stop him, Josh sauntered right up to the lady and leaned against the railing like some suave leading man in a movie.

Chapter 3

Lacy

"BEAUTIFUL VIEW, ISN'T IT?" a male voice drawled to the right of me.

Hoping the guy wasn't talking to me, I glanced in his direction, then jerked upright. It was the fake-celebrity guy, still dressed in that glaring Hawaiian shirt and slacks, leaning against the railing like he owned the boat and I was his personal guest.

It took me a second to remember he had asked a question. "Yes."

He smiled, obviously pleased by my startled reaction. The man was used to his charm getting everything he wanted. The hatred for my dad rose up, so I faced the ocean, not wanting to give him another ounce of success. Why in the world was he picking me of all people—

Oh, I was standing by myself. I was practically screaming easy prey. Still, I wasn't the type that usually attracted guys like him. So why would he be hitting on me?

Wait. My dad was brought down by an overly good-looking woman in a sting operation. What if this guy was with the police and was here to ferret out my secrets? It might be a far-fetched scenario, but I could never be too sure. I still remembered how I had assumed the cute blonde woman my father was head over heels with might end up being my new mom. Instead, she sent us to jail. Yeah, that betrayal still stung.

"You here all by yourself?" he asked.

The desire to spit out a lie, that I had an intimidating boyfriend who would show up any moment to tell him to back off, nearly leaped out of my mouth, but I caught it in time. I already had enough lies haunting me. I had to be honest, especially if this was a sting operation.

"I am, but if you're looking for a frilly thing to pass the time with, I'm not your girl." Probably a bit too mean, but hey, it was honest.

His grin widened. "You saying I'm not your type?"

I eased an inch away from him. His smile was too much like my dad's when he was about to succeed in manipulating someone. I was tired of fake men and manipulation. I wanted to be treated as an equal, not as some chess piece for their personal game.

I arched an eyebrow and hoped I looked bored. I'd seen prettier women do this to shoot down a guy's advances. "I have a feeling you don't actually care what my answer will be."

His charming smile cracked for a moment, but it re-ignited when a group of girls walked by, their excited giggles escalating when he flashed his rows of flawless, white teeth at them.

I bit back a gag. "Have a good day, sir."

His attention shot back to me. "You're right," he drawled. "I don't care what your answer will be. However"—he put his back against the railing and tilted his head to the right—"he would care."

I followed the direction he indicated and spotted an equally attractive man with dark chestnut hair. He was dressed in a polo and slacks and occupied a chair less than fifty feet from me. His look of dismay and worry instantly dried up when I caught his gaze and he ducked his head, but not before I spotted the embarrassed flush.

"So?" the fake-celebrity guy asked, still leaning against the railing as if he had all day to annoy me. "Up to rejecting a second man in as many minutes?"

I leveled my eyes on him. "I wasn't rejecting you, just indicating I'm not interested."

He grinned. "That's the same thing, lady. And while I don't care—"

"That's obvious."

"*He* would care. Do me a favor and talk to him. If you don't like him, just walk away after two minutes. I can let him down gentler than you can." His cocky tone had softened.

Even though I knew he was manipulating me, I had a hunch the fake celebrity really did care for his friend. I eyed the shy guy again. He stared so hard at the laptop on his lap, it looked like he wanted to dive into it and I bit back a laugh. It was rather cute to see a guy so nervous—the complete opposite of my dad.

"All right, but"—I waved a finger at the fake celebrity—"this will be the *only* favor I do for you. Try this again and you will be disappointed."

He nodded with an amused grin. "Yes, ma'am."

I strode over to the shy one and stuck out my hand. "Hi. Your friend here says you like me." Oops, probably shouldn't have been that honest. Oh well.

He shot a glare at his friend, who instantly raised his hands in defense. "Those were not my exact words."

"True," I said. "But you can't deny it was your implication."

The fake celebrity gave a mock bow. "I would never deny anything to a beautiful woman." He then raised his arm and checked a wrist devoid of any gadgets. "Look at the time; I must go. Have fun!" He clapped the shy guy on the back, then sauntered off, no doubt to annoy another unsuspecting female.

The shy guy cleared his throat. "Uh, sorry about him. He can be... a handful."

"I noticed."

"And, for the record, I did not ask him to be my wingman. I told him I wasn't interested but he just charged on his own."

I arched an eyebrow. "Not interested, you say? So what is this all about, then?"

His eyes widened and he worked his jaw for a second as if desperate to say something but he couldn't decide on what.

It was both disturbing and heartwarming to see a man so floundered by my presence. Still, I didn't like making someone so uncomfortable. "You can say whatever is on your mind."

He stared up at me. "You're very blunt."

I shrugged. "I prefer being honest. I don't like it when someone says one thing but means another."

He smiled and I had to bite back a gasp. It lit up his brown eyes, turning them into mounds of chocolate. "I agree wholeheartedly with that." The tension in his body eased a little but he stared at his hands as if unsure of what to do next. He really was shy.

And I liked that.

"Is this your first cruise?" I asked.

He laughed. "No, I'm afraid not. I go on this particular cruise at least once every year."

"Where you practice picking up women on the first day?" I couldn't help saying. Like I hoped, he immediately flushed. He was cute when embarrassed.

"That was Josh's idea—"

"I was teasing."

"Oh." A rueful laugh escaped his lips. "I guess I'm used to serious people."

"Your friend, Josh, can be serious?"

He glanced up at me as if he was catching on to my jokes. "Only when forced."

I laughed. "I could believe that."

"I take it this is your first cruise?" he asked.

"Am I that obvious?"

He indicated the wide expanse of water before us. "You kept gazing at the ocean as if you'd never seen it before."

So, he had been watching me for a while. The fact made me slightly nervous. I wasn't used to being noticed. It was an ability my dad had used to his advantage since no one ever paid me much attention.

"I spent most of my life in the middle of the country, but I've seen the ocean a few times. But"—I turned my head toward the rolling blue water and breathed in the salty air—"there's something about those waters that just draws you in, you know?"

"Yeah," his voice was soft and I turned, expecting his eyes to be on the ocean as well, but his dark eyes were on me. "I completely agree."

I gulped as the reality that this good-looking, no doubt wealthy man might actually be interested in me hit me hard. I had always wanted to find love—good, strong love, the type I saw in movies but never in real life—but I despaired it would happen to me. Not with my past. I either had to lie and evade every question regarding my upbringing or pray the guy wouldn't drop me the second he learned about my father and my early years of crime. And I had a hunch this guy would do the latter. He might be shy, but he had access to much higher-quality women than me.

I forced a smile. "Well, it was nice meeting you, but I should go."

The disappointment was obvious on his face. Maybe I should stay.

No, once he knew my past, he would be gone. And I didn't need that pain.

"Thanks for chatting with me," he said. "Maybe we'll run into each other again."

"It's possible." That was all I dared to say before walking away. I counted up to thirty steps before I darted a glance in his direction—only to catch his eyes. He had been watching me the entire time!

Embarrassed, I hurried out of sight, constantly reminding myself that fairytale endings didn't happen to me. They just didn't.

David

I watched her walk away, sadness settling deep inside me. I didn't even know why I was so disappointed. It wasn't like it was going to work out anyway—I had made a fool of myself, as always.

Still, it was disturbing to be so intrigued by someone I barely knew. She had such a strange mix of bold confidence and nervous anxiety, like she knew her worth but was terrified someone was going to see it, that I couldn't keep my eyes off her. I wished she'd look back, that she'd give me some hope that I had something of a chance. Not that I wanted it—

She suddenly looked back, those piercing blue eyes catching mine for a second before she disappeared around the corner.

Never mind. I definitely wanted to meet her again.

Wait, what was I thinking? I didn't have time for this. I had a thief to catch before my father realized the mess I had made of his company.

I focused on the screen of my laptop, but instead of seeing the spreadsheet, I could only see the woman's teasing smile. I wished I had been quicker to pick up on her wit. She might have stayed longer if she'd seen I had more intelligence than my sputtering tongue could deliver.

"What did you do?" Josh asked, appearing out of nowhere. Had he been watching this whole time? "Why is she gone?"

"She said she had to go," I said. "The bags should have been delivered to the rooms by now. She probably went to go check on that." It was the first explanation I could come up with.

"A girl doesn't up and leave to go check her bag," Josh shot back. "I should have stuck around and saved you from messing it up."

"Wow, thanks for the vote of confidence," I muttered and hunkered lower in the chair. "Now maybe you'll regret forcing me out of my suite."

"Not in the least. What did she say? Did you get her name?"

I grimaced. "I completely forgot."

"Did she at least stay longer than two minutes?"

"Oh, I'm sorry. Next time you force a girl on me, Josh, I will start my timer so I know exactly how long it takes before I frighten them off."

"That's not what I meant. I'm just trying to figure out how much damage control I need to do."

"For the sake of my pride, I must state she did look back when she walked away."

Josh's whole demeanor changed. "She looked back?" He clapped me on the shoulder. "That's great! I can work with that."

I shook off his hand. "Please don't. You've already made me look like a fool, then shot dead my confidence. I don't need your help burying what's left of my pride."

Josh grinned. "Come on, David. You can do this. Besides, I'm just helping you to break up with your laptop. It's been trying to tell you to move on for a long time now."

I pulled my laptop closer to me. "I'll have you know that my laptop and I have a very good understanding."

"That is very sad to hear," Josh said. "You know what? You should skip the meeting tonight. Stay on this deck and see if she'll show up again. Then make sure you get her name!"

"I will not blow off that meeting for some random girl."

"David, where is your spirit of adventure? Of romance?"

"I run a company, Josh, and these are my employees, the ones who did exceptionally well this year."

"Yeah, like skimming off three million from their favorite boss."

I growled at the thought of it. "That is another reason I can't dump everything to chase some girl."

Josh waved it off. "I'll have her confessing before we reach the first island. You just need to relax and get this new girl's name."

"No," I stated, focusing back on my laptop.

Josh shook his head. "See, this is why you can't keep a girl around. You fail to make them feel special."

"And you keep them around better?" I shot back.

"I leave them behind. I don't get left behind. There's a difference."

I shook my head. "I really don't think I should be taking romantic advice from a man who prides himself on how many broken hearts he's caused."

"It's better than trying to coax a romance out of that laptop of yours."

I groaned. "Don't you have someone else to annoy?"

"Nope," he said. "But I'm sure I can find someone."

"Then please do."

"Gladly!" Josh said, sauntering off.

Chapter 4

Lacy

I STARED AT THE image of me in the mirror, holding two outfits against my body. One was a flirty, scarlet dress, the one I had bought when my fake name had become real. I had wanted to celebrate the new me, but then never gathered the nerve to wear it.

The eyes of that shy man crossed my mind. I wondered how wide they'd get if I wore this around him.

No, I wasn't wearing it for him. I had a meeting to attend. One where I would meet David Wellington, the man who would hopefully believe my story and not send me to jail.

I focused on the other outfit, a simple dress shirt and black slacks; my version of casual business. Before this whole mess of the stolen millions, I had imagined wearing this to prove I was someone to be taken seriously and ready to rise up in the company. Now it might look like I was trying too hard to not look guilty. But, if I went with the flirty dress, it might come across as though I was hoping to seduce David into believing me.

That made the decision for me and I changed into the sensible business casual outfit. It might not impress anyone, but at least no one could accuse me of acting like my dad.

I focused on making my maybe-wavy brown hair have a little more spunk, touched up my makeup, then gazed over the finished presentation. My outfit was definitely sensible, but the expression in my eyes was like a deer caught in the headlights. Why was I never good at hiding how I felt?

I stepped toward the round window situated in the middle of the far wall, but my suite was on the side that faced the harbor and while we were slowly pulling from it, the view just wasn't as calming as the endless blue waters.

The urge to call Sarah popped up, but I didn't have the time. Taking a deep breath, I smoothed down my hair, grabbed my purse and keycard, and then headed down the hallway for the elevators. Arriving on the main floor, I checked the map on my phone and headed in the direction I believed was correct. Except I found myself passing the casino room—that meant I had gone the wrong direction. A sense of direction had never been a strong point of mine, even with maps.

I turned around but happened to glance through the windows of the casino room. Though the room was dark—it wouldn't open until we were in international waters—memories of my earlier years flooded in. The smoky haze, the racket of dings and trills from the machines, and my mother's legs swinging as she sat on the chair, her bleary eyes consumed by the colorful game before her. The most interaction I got from her on those days was when she would let me pull the lever. It was funny how I had once thought it was normal to spend days sitting by my mother as she played those dumb games. It never occurred to me to wonder why there were no other children also bored out of their minds.

I shook the memory away. I had been too young when my mother passed away to understand how much she had lacked in the mothering department. Now that I was older, I didn't want the hate I had for one parent to bleed to the other. She had not been a great example but I still wanted to love her, and the best way to do that was to avoid most of my memories about her.

Returning to the elevators, I orientated myself with the map on the wall against the map on my phone. Once I confirmed the correct direction, I made my way down the other hallway, ignoring the doors that led outside to where I'd find the sea—and maybe that cute guy.

No, no cute guy. I didn't get happy endings with potentially rich guys, remember? And I was about to face several people who believed I was no better than my swindling father. If I couldn't get them to believe me, this was going to be my last vacation. I didn't know how long someone would get for stealing three million dollars, but I had a feeling it would be longer than the two years I spent last time.

A couple pushed through the doors leading out into the deck and I stiffened, recognizing both at once. The petite blonde hanging on to the middle-aged man was Izzy, a clingy co-worker in a different department who I preferred to avoid. The man, Gabe, had also been a co-worker when I had first begun working, two clerks desperate to rise up the ranks. Despite the fifteen years between us, we had become friends, trading jokes during the long, tedious hours. But once he earned a promotion, I was no longer good enough and the friendship dried up.

The look of distaste consumed his face like it always did when he saw me. "Lacy. I wasn't expecting to see you here."

Gabe was now my boss's boss's boss. Yeah, he had moved up a lot in the past five years. I hadn't begrudged him since he was a hard worker—and I knew he needed the funds since he was a single dad raising three kids—but that didn't mean he had to be so rude to me.

"I got promoted," I said. Gabe wasn't like Kevin, attentive to details, and I was pretty sure he had failed to keep tabs on me. "And I designed the new macros the accounting department uses." It was the reason I had been given a spot on the coveted company retreat. I had developed those codes over a year ago but hadn't dared show them off until my fake name was in place and I didn't have to worry about a spotlight being shined on me. Too bad that worry of mine had ended up being a complete waste.

The look of surprise the news generated on his face emboldened my polite smile.

"Well," he said with a slight cough, "that explains much."

My smile wilted. What was that supposed to mean?

"What are macros?" Izzy piped up.

Gabe coughed. "They're a way to automate tasks in programs we use in the Accounting department." He waved a hand at me. "Lacy, this is Izzy. She—"

Izzy giggled. "Oh, she knows me! I hang out with her and Sarah all the time!"

She *tried* to hang out with us would be more accurate, though she did succeed with Sarah more often. They both loved to shop; I didn't.

"I'm so excited you're here, too!" Izzy continued. "I think we're going to be the only two girls on this retreat. We should do something girly together to celebrate female power, maybe like do a spa day together?"

I didn't have a lot of money to spend on this cruise—and now had even less if I had to pay for a lawyer—but Gabe cut in before I could object.

"I wouldn't make such firm plans quite yet," he said, the look of distaste strong in his eyes. "Lacy might be getting off for good at the first stop."

My stomach dropped to my shoes. He knew. It must have been Gabe that Kevin had been on the phone with. That would make sense. Gabe was a senior in the company now and would have direct access to David, the CEO.

"Plans can change," I shot back. "Now, if you'll excuse me, I have something to do." I skirted around them and marched out of the hallway and onto the deck. Once I reached the railing, I mentally cursed myself. What was I thinking, lying? We were all supposed to attend that welcome meeting—of course I had nothing else to do but head in the same direction as them. But no, I panicked and resorted to lying just to get away from Gabe.

Lies. I hated them, yet seemed to resort to them all the time. When was I going to find a life where I didn't need them so much?

And the line Gabe had said—that the first stop in Key West might be my last. The Keys were still the USA—a warrant for my arrest could easily be issued there. And with my little white lie, I had carved another black mark against me. Who was going to believe me when I couldn't stick to plain honesty in the first place?

I plopped my head into my hands. How in the world was I going to get myself out of this?

"You okay?" a male voice asked.

I whipped my head up, then froze as my eyes took in that cute, shy guy, a hesitant smile on his face as if he wasn't sure how well I would react to his bold move. And wow, he was tall. I had assumed so despite him sitting last time we had met, but seeing him tower over me was a bit much. He had to be hitting six feet at least. Nor did it help that he wore a suit, tailored to emphasize those broad shoulders of his.

"Uh, h-hi," I stuttered like some brainless female.

His smile withered. "Sorry, I didn't mean to startle you."

My emotions were all over the place. I wanted to be left alone to panic, but I didn't want him to go away. The latter might be irrational, but

I didn't want to be rational. Shoving down my feelings of despair, I plastered on what I hoped was a sweet smile. "It's, uh, okay; my mind was elsewhere."

"I noticed." He leaned against the railing, only a couple of inches from me. Despite the salty air, I caught a whiff of his cologne and I was pretty sure it was the expensive kind. No way he could smell that good on a supermarket budget.

"Did you get some bad news?" he asked.

Lots of bad news, but I wasn't going to blurt that out to a complete stranger. I might only have one night on this ship and I didn't want the one guy in years who had noticed me to learn of the hot mess he was trying to get to know. But neither did I want to lie and insist everything was fine. I was done with lying.

"I can't swim," I blurted out instead.

He seemed confused for a second, but it cleared once he looked out at the ocean. "You said this was your first time on a cruise."

"Yes."

"And you're freaking out that we might sink?"

"It is a possibility." It was the closest thing I could get to the truth.

"Well, I've taken this exact cruise every year for nearly a decade. And since I have no cool story to tell of almost dying on a sinking ship, I think you'll be safe."

I blinked for a second, then laughed. It just bubbled out of me. Only Sarah had ever been able to get me to laugh when I was stressed out. "Well, you never know. This might be the year that ruins your streak."

"You saying you're bad luck?"

I was a black hole of bad luck, but I just shrugged. "Let's just say I've watched too many movies and the boat always sinks at the end."

He chuckled. "You make a good point. Luckily for us, we're not in a movie, so I'm pretty sure we're going to be okay. But, if it makes you feel better, I'm a really good swimmer. I'll make sure you're okay."

My heart melted. He didn't know me at all and yet was offering to keep me safe. I had always wanted someone to look out for me, to be there when the world caved in. Oh, why did my life have to be such a mess that I couldn't end up with a guy like him?

Scared I might start saying something sappy, I shot out a question, "How did you learn to swim so well?"

"My first job was being a lifeguard at my community pool. Did that for three years."

I struggled to not let my jaw drop in shock. With the amount of money he had blown on that suit, I had assumed he must have grown up in some fancy house with a private pool—maybe even a private beach. But not only did he go to a community center, he also worked there?

He grinned. "Bet you didn't expect that."

I laughed. "Yeah, sorry. You got me on that one."

"To be fair, it was really for my younger sister. She had a bad experience when she was a toddler and was terrified of the water. I became a lifeguard so she would feel safe."

My heart was fast becoming a puddle of mushy sappiness. Not only was he a good guy, but a caring brother. Why was I meeting such a perfect guy just days before I ended up in jail again?

"What about you?" he asked. "Have any siblings?"

My heart hardened at once at the dreaded question of my family. "I'm afraid my non-existent brother wasn't there to teach me how to swim," I said instead.

"That's too bad. What about your sister?"

I shook my head. "I'm an only child. Do you have more than one sister?" I countered, desperate to avoid the topic of my parents. I really, really didn't want to lie to him.

"I have two sisters," he answered. "Both are younger than me, but I'm closer to Jane. She's the youngest one."

"She more fun?"

He shook his head. "She's not as afraid of me as Megan is."

"Afraid?" Maybe I shouldn't be falling for this guy so fast. "Are you actually a terror of a brother?"

"No. I'm just... a lot like my father, I guess. And he and Megan never really have gotten along."

"Oh." I could understand a rift with a parent. "Well, I don't know your dad, but you seem nice enough to me.

He grinned, lighting up those gorgeous brown eyes. "You think I'm nice?"

I flushed. "W-well, so far. I reserve the right to change my mind."

He laughed at that. "Sounds fair. I'm David, by the way." He extended his hand. "I should have mentioned that earlier; sorry about that."

I accepted his hand. "I'm Lacy."

His expression of eager interest changed as if alarmed and confused.

"Something the matter?" I asked. I had picked that name myself—what was wrong with it?

He released my hand. "No, sorry. I just know another Lacy."

"Ex-girlfriend?" The question slipped out before I could stop it.

He shook his head. "No, just... not a good person."

"Well, Lacy is a common name, so don't assume everyone with that name is bad. I mean, I know a few Davids, too, but I didn't immediately assume you were like them."

He quirked an eyebrow at me. "Ex-boyfriend?"

Oh, he had used the same trap on me. Smart kid. "Nope. One is a neighbor of mine. Grumpy fellow. Please don't be like him. Another was a very nice store employee who helped me out. You can be like him. And the other is my boss. Well, my boss's, boss's, boss's, I-forget-how-many-levels-there-are-boss." That last part was meant as a joke, but he didn't smile. In fact, that look of alarm returned.

"What is his last name?"

I suddenly remembered that rich people were a small group. It was possible this David knew my boss David.

"I should mention that I never said my boss was bad or anything," I shot out. "I've never even met him personally. I just know him by reputation and he seems to be a good guy."

"What's his name?" There was an edge to his voice now.

What type of a boss was my boss? "David Wellington. Do you know him?"

His face hardened as though he was shutting down all emotion. "Excuse me." He stepped around me and headed for the doors I had used to get onto the deck.

I stared after him in shock. What had that been all about?

A second later, I realized I was now super late for the company meeting.

Dashing into the hallway, I hurried toward the ballroom. To my surprise, I spotted David going in the same direction. A heavy sense of dread formed in my stomach, but it didn't erupt until David, the nice one that I thought could possibly like me for who I really was, entered the same ballroom that I was headed toward.

Well, my mind griped, at least I knew now why he'd backed off so fast.

Chapter 5

David

My father used to always say that if a problem hit you and you didn't know what to do, ditch all emotion and stick to the facts.

I was doing exactly that as I rattled out the niceties and information for the welcoming meeting of the fifty employees and the plus ones they had brought along. Usually, I kept my talk short—less than fifteen minutes—and then let my employees mingle and enjoy the light buffet at the back of the room. But I knew the second I sat down, I would have to deal with the fact that the intriguing girl I'd been obsessing over for the past few hours was the one and only Lacy Armstrong, the smug thief who had stolen millions from me.

Had the whole thing been a trap? A ploy for her to sink her claws into me and twist me to do her bidding? But she had seemed so honest—so genuine! But then again, I had never dealt with a professional swindler. She must have read somewhere that I didn't do well with flirtatious women. That might be why she projected this more honest version of a woman.

And I had nearly fallen for it.

I checked the clock and realized I'd eaten up thirty minutes, double my usual time. And I could see Gabe, one of my best employees, trying hard to check a yawn. I needed to quit or I'd be setting a bad start for this company retreat.

"Thanks, everyone," I announced. "Please, stay and enjoy the food at the back. If it's not enough, the dinner buffet will open in another hour. You can gorge yourself then."

There was light laughter at my lame attempt at a joke and yet, the whole group converged on the buffet as if it was their last chance for food. It always amazed me how much people would obsess over free food. The thief, however, remained in her seat, her eyes on me like some predator. I still couldn't believe I fell so easily for her. I had even been late for my own meeting when I spotted her leaning against the railing. She had looked so distraught—I had wanted to cheer her up. But now I see it had been a ruse to get me to care about her.

"That was long," Josh said as he stepped toward me. "I never imagined you'd have so many random facts about cruises stored in that head of yours."

"I just wanted to be thorough," I countered. Out of the corner of my eye, I kept tabs on the thief—I refused to use her name. I needed as much mental distance as possible.

"No one would accuse you of not doing that. But I have a feeling that's not the real reason you went on for so long." Josh's eyes darted in the direction of the thief.

"That's Lacy Armstrong." I kept my voice low.

Josh's eyebrows show up. "Really?" He lowered them, an intrigued smile on his lips. "Well, this just got a whole lot more interesting."

"You going to talk to her now?" I was totally gung-ho for Josh to do what he does best now. I had never wanted someone ruined as much as I wanted Lacy destroyed at this moment. She had robbed me blind, then rubbed salt in the wound by humiliating me.

"I can do that. But let's just wait for a second."

I balked. "Why?"

"'Cause she's coming to us."

I turned, ready to bolt, but she was standing right there in front of me. Nervous apprehension arrested her face, but a bold determination steadied her eyes. My sister, Megan, would look like that when she was about to challenge my father on something.

"Hi," she began, staring straight at me, but Josh leaned toward her, diverting her attention.

"Hello, gorgeous," he said as if he meant it. Sometimes, I was amazed at how well Josh could hide his true feelings. "I don't think I ever learned your name."

"Lacy," she answered, her eyes back on me.

The urge to call out that lie sprung to my lips, but I bit it back. She had no idea I knew she had robbed me. In fact, I shouldn't be acting so cold to her—I was going to alarm her and then she'd disappear the second we parked at the first island.

"You here to ask advice on what activities would be the most fun when we reach Key West?" Josh asked. "I'd advise snorkeling. Best thing to do, hands down."

I opened my mouth to let Josh know she couldn't swim, but then snapped it shut. I had no idea how true that statement was.

She scrunched her eyebrows together. "I don't know what snorkeling is."

"Really?" Josh asked, taking a closer step to her. I noted she took a step back, maintaining a safe distance from him. She must be recognizing his game. I wasn't surprised. They both had sharpened skills to charm their victims.

"Allow me to enlighten you," Josh continued as if she hadn't moved at all. "It's where you get a close-up view of the many species of fishes."

"Oh, like an aquarium?"

"Aquariums are boring. Snorkeling is more fun. You'll love it. You should come."

"Is it, um, included?" she asked.

"It is," I lied.

She looked at me. "Will you be going?"

Josh draped an arm around my shoulders. "Of course! It's one of his favorite activities!"

She didn't seem entirely thrilled, but who knew if that was her real emotion. "Okay. I'll come."

"Perfect," Josh said. "I'll sign us up and then pick you up at your cabin, say, at nine a.m.?"

She shook her head as well as took another step away from him. "I can figure it out on my own, thanks." She faced me again. "I—"

"Excuse me," Gabe said, surprising all three of us. "But Izzy has a question for Lacy. Lacy?"

A slightly sour expression fell over Lacy's face but was quickly dispelled with a polite smile. "Of course. Excuse me." She moved away and I fully expected Gabe to follow, but he turned to me.

"Sorry, boss. I didn't know she'd be so bold as to approach you directly."

I waved his concern aside. "Don't worry about me. Go and enjoy your vacation."

He nodded. "Will do. Thanks, boss."

Josh lifted an eyebrow at me. "He knows?"

"Yeah, he and one other, but he's the only one on this ship who knows."

"I wish he hadn't intervened," Josh said, his eyes on the mingling crowd. I was fully aware of exactly where the thief was, but Josh's gaze didn't seem to be singling her out.

"Why?" I asked. I was actually relieved. Unlike Josh, I wasn't practiced in the art of masking my emotions.

"Because I would have liked to have had the ten minutes alone with her as I walked her to the activity tomorrow. And, while we're on that topic, why did you claim it was included?"

I opened my mouth for a second, then closed it. "Come with me." I headed back into the hallway, Josh following close behind. But I didn't say anything until we were out on the deck and I knew no one was following us.

"She told me she couldn't swim. I want to see if that statement is true."

Josh raised an eyebrow. "So, what? You're going to toss her into the ocean and see if she drowns? I thought that was how our ancestors determined if someone was a witch, not a liar."

"I was a lifeguard for three years. I can tell if someone can swim or not."

"Won't we all be wearing life jackets?"

"Doesn't matter. Someone who can't swim will swim a lot differently in a life jacket than someone who knows what they're doing."

"That still doesn't explain why you claimed it was included when it obviously is not."

"I didn't want her to back out by pretending she didn't have the money." Despite stealing so much from me, she didn't dress like she could afford much. Probably another part of her scam.

"So, you're going to stick her with the bill?"

A good part of me wanted to say yes, but the lessons my father had drilled into me screamed against it. "I'll pay for it. I don't want her to think I lied. Then I'll be no better than she."

"But you claimed it was a part of the company retreat. She's going to figure out you lied about that."

"Then she can think her plan is working and she's twisting me around her finger as planned."

Josh abruptly grinned. "And here I thought you'd never do well at the subterfuge game."

"She stole three million, Josh, then tried to get all friendly on me as if I were an idiot. I will do everything in my power to make sure she's caught and locked away for a long time."

"Well, while you're in the mood to open that incredible tight wallet of yours, how about getting me my own suite?"

I scoffed. "You can afford to get it yourself."

"I already tried." The whine was obvious in his voice. "There's no room."

That would explain why he was miffed at the check-in counter earlier. "So why are you asking me to try to get you one?"

"Well, there are lower cabins available..."

I rolled my eyes. "You are not forcing me out of my own suite."

"But you hardly enjoy it! I, on the other hand, would do it justice!"

I gave him a deadpan stare. "It's not happening. Ever."

He sighed. "Now I really wish I had those ten minutes with Lacy."

I eyed him. "Why?"

"'Cause then maybe *she* will convince you to give me that suite."

The thought of her trying to cozy up to me again made me clench my fists. "The only thing that girl is going to get out of me is prison."

Chapter 6

Lacy

I KEPT A SMILE in place as Izzy chatted about the food, insisting she wanted to know my opinion if the chocolate fondue was better than at our company's annual parties.

"I think this one here is a lot better. I think we should convince Gabe to find out how they made it so good, then get it for this year's party. What do you think?"

"Sounds good," I said, my eyes on David as he and Josh walked out of the room. So much for my grand plan to get him alone and explain my situation. I could still remember the coldness in his brown eyes, like frozen, mangled dirt. He hated me. And that hurt. A lot.

But, he believed I had stolen three million. I'd hate that person too.

I half wondered if I could get Gabe to let me see the data—maybe I could figure out who had actually done it. But I knew Gabe would call the cops first if I dared try that. And David would do the exact same, assuming I could get close enough to him to even ask. I had a feeling he was going to keep me as far away from him as possible, no doubt assuming that I was doing my father's tricks and trying to seduce him. The thought made me gag.

"I thought you said it was good?" Izzy asked.

I grimaced. My face must be displaying all of my inner turmoil. "No, the chocolate is good. I was just thinking how much I'm going to regret the calorie-fest later."

Izzy giggled. "Don't I know that pain! I'm going to have to work out to so many videos next week. But it's going to be worth it." She bit into a chocolate-covered strawberry and savored it loudly.

"What activity are you doing tomorrow?" she asked as she patted her red lips clean of the chocolate.

"Snorkeling, I think."

Her eyes went wide. "Oh, me too! And Gabe! This will be so much fun. But make sure you put on a lot of sunscreen. Last time, I forgot and I was so red all over my back that it hurt for a whole week! Don't make the same mistake; trust me."

I eyed her. "What were you wearing that you got burned all over your back? Aren't aquariums inside?"

She cocked her head. "Inside? You sweet thing, do you not know what snorkeling is?"

"Something where you see a lot of fish?"

She laughed for a full ten seconds and I regretted asking her anything.

"You are so funny!" She brushed tears from her eyes. "Snorkeling is when you go out to where the fish are and you swim around with them."

I coughed on the chocolate I was trying to swallow. "Swim? You have to swim to snorkel?"

"Oh! Do you not know how to swim?"

I shook my head. And David should have known. Had he not remembered? Or did he do it on purpose, hoping I'd drown? Maybe he wasn't so nice after all. Which was devastating news—that meant he would never bother to believe me.

"Don't worry, sweetie." She grabbed my hand and gave it a squeeze. "Truth is, I can't swim worth beans, either."

"How'd you survive?"

She broke into another fit of giggles. I had no idea how Gabe could stand her.

"You are so funny, Lacy! I just know we're going to be the best of friends."

I hoped not. I was already looking for the nearest exit.

"Snorkeling doesn't require you to swim. You wear these ugly orange jacket things. It totally clashes with your swimsuit, but they insist on it. And then, for those of us not good in the water, you can hang onto this big white circle thing and the instructor guy, he takes you out to where the fish are. You don't have to swim one stroke. It's great."

"Are you sure?"

"Yeah. Don't worry one thing about it. Trust me."

But I had one other problem. "I didn't bring a swimsuit." I didn't even own one.

"Oh, we must fix that! You need something very cute if you want to catch David."

I nearly dropped my cup. "What?"

She winked at me and leaned toward me. "Don't worry," she whispered in a conspiratorial tone. "I'd go for him myself if Gabe wasn't such a dream already. But a multi-billionaire that young and hot?" She fanned herself. "They should have laws against that!"

I pulled away from her. "I have no intention of *catching* our boss."

"Why not? This company is okay with dating bosses as long as he's not directly over you and since David works at headquarters and in a different state, him being a boss shouldn't count."

"Yes, it does. I'm, uh, pretty full now. I'm going to head back to my room."

I began pardoning my way through the crowd while Izzy cried out, "But we need to go shopping!"

I didn't bother to reply. My focus was just to get out of that room. To think Izzy immediately assumed me talking to David meant I was trying to nab him like he was some object to grab. It sounded too much like how my dad would speak of his next prey. I was never, ever, going to do that to anyone.

The next morning found me in the gift shops on the ship, desperately trying to find a swimsuit I could afford. I just needed something cheap for the one-time use, but the prices were excessive and eye-popping. There was no way I was going to pay that much for an activity I had been duped into going to. The more I thought about it, the more I was sure this whole thing was a test. David must be wanting to see if I really couldn't swim. Well, he was going to learn that I definitely did not lie about that. Just thinking about being in the water was causing me to hyperventilate. But Izzy had survived, and she didn't know how to swim. That had to mean something. And David had insisted he had once been a lifeguard. He wouldn't let me drown, right? Or was he some twisted killer, intending on killing me instead of taking me to court?

Well, I certainly wasn't going to drown in an overly priced, barely there frilly outfit. I resorted to asking a clerk for help. She immediately assured me that I didn't need a swimsuit, but anything I already owned that I was okay with getting wet would suffice.

That brought me to my next dilemma. What did I own that I was willing to be seen completely drenched in? A white-anything on top was definitely out. I rifled through the clothes I had brought, trying to deduce the damage that seawater might bring to them. I finally decided on a faded pair of shorts and my oldest shirt. I had originally planned to only wear them while I lounged in the privacy of my cabin, but desperate measures called for desperate solutions. Donning the not-so-flattering outfit, I did find solace in one thing. Izzy couldn't dare claim I was trying to catch anyone in this old thing.

I focused on my hair. Water tended to make the undecided-wavy strands of my hair frizz. And I had no idea how to not make that happen. This whole thing was going to end with me in a humiliating mess. But, hopefully, David would finally trust me and would believe me when I told him I wasn't the one who had stolen from him.

In resignation, I threw my hair into a ponytail, located my sunglasses, then headed out to where the snorkeling party would debark from. Unfortunately, everyone else seemed to have picked the same time to debark and I found myself in a long line to head out. Just great. Now I would probably miss the activity and David would think I chickened out and he'd, no doubt, see it as proof I was guilty.

"Lacy!"

I jerked in shock, then fought hard not to recoil as Josh moved toward me, dressed in another outrageous Hawaiian shirt of competing bright reds and yellows which he had also paired with blue shorts. His arms and legs, however, were covered by a light yellow spandex material. Maybe it was some sort of strange fashion for the rich?

"It's to protect my skin," Josh said, apparently having caught my confused gaze. "Skin cancer runs in my family," he added as if that explained anything. "You should invest in some yourself. Don't want your lovely skin ruined by the sun's rays over time."

He let his eyes run over my body, but I couldn't believe his expression of pleasure for one second. I knew very well that I was not attractive in this outfit, and none of his fake charm was going to convince me otherwise. All his attention was doing was making me wish I had worn a parka instead.

"I applied sunblock," I said. "Why are you here?" I didn't want to deal with Josh. I just wanted to survive the snorkeling and then somehow pull David aside and convince him I wasn't the culprit. "I'm sure there's a VIP line for you."

"And I'm here to take you through it, of course." He offered his arm and it took me a second to realize he wanted me to thread my hand into the nook of his elbow.

He needed a prettier woman than me to be on his arm. "I'm okay, thanks. I can wait."

"Don't be absurd." His arm was around my waist before I could object and he pulled me forward. I resisted once, but the strength in his arm and muscular body was no match for me. I'd have to start kicking and screaming to get him to stop. Not wanting to cause a scene, I obeyed, but not after shooting him a glare.

"This is under protest."

"Of course it is." That was all he said as he steered me toward a more private exit off the boat, passing by a security guard who waved us on without hesitation.

"Isn't it nice having perks?" Josh beamed.

I had had such perks before, back when my dad pursued ladies with deep pockets and pricey connections. And I couldn't forget the undercover cop who had wooed my dad. She'd showered us with perks like these. If Josh hadn't shown up like he was a rock star on that first day, I would have begun to bet he was operating a sting operation and I was his target.

"Depends on the price." I pushed his arm off me and, thankfully, he complied.

"There's our car." He indicated an SUV waiting at the curb. A man stepped out of the driver's side and hurried around to open the back door for us. But no one was inside.

I stopped dead in my tracks, my suspicious mind on overdrive. The idea of him taking me somewhere where I'd never return screamed inside me. I barely knew Josh and while he seemed very buddy-buddy with

David, that didn't mean he was a good man. The fact that he acted so much like my father only heightened my fear.

"Where is everyone else?" I demanded.

He laughed. "Relax, you're going to be fine. Key West isn't big enough to hide a body anyway."

I shot him a glare. Was he teasing? With those eyes filled with giddy amusement? Yes, he was. He seemed to enjoy making me uneasy.

"Everyone is already at the boat," he continued. "You were late, so I came back to see what was taking you so long."

"The flyer said to be at the dock at ten a.m.," I said, pulling out my phone. I still had ten minutes and I was at the dock already.

"The dock for the snorkeling boat, and that's five minutes away." He indicated the SUV, the chauffeur guy still waiting with the opened door. "Ready?"

"That means I'll still be on time," I shot back as I climbed in the vehicle, then scooted to the far end. Josh, however, planted himself in the middle, sitting right next to me. I ignored him and stared out the window. With the stress of dealing with Josh, I hadn't been able to take in the gorgeous scenery around me. I had never been on a small island and it amazed me that it could be filled with so many people.

The drive was short, as promised, and I didn't wait for the chauffeur to open the door but practically leaped out by myself and found myself in front of a shop with signs boasting of their marvelous snorkeling tours. I scanned for David or Izzy, but only found several employees of the store as well as the ever-annoying Josh.

"This way," he said and I reluctantly followed him down a ramp heading toward a small boat. I gulped. We were going to go in that? It seemed so tiny in comparison with the cruise boat and it rolled back and forth as if about to tip over.

"Lacy!" Izzy cried and I breathed a sigh of relief, hoping Josh would switch to her now. But then I took in her outfit. She wore one of the barely-there bikinis I had perused on the cruise ship, but she had the perfect body for it. And I knew without one doubt that the other three guys standing in a circle around her, including Gabe, were going to compare me in my dowdy outfit. Normally, I wouldn't care, but I was already outside my element and I didn't need another reminder that I didn't belong in this group.

Then my eyes fell on David, standing a bit off from the three other guys and Izzy. He wore the same spandex shirt as Josh, but it seemed to make his muscles look as if carved in stone. The man was built—and I was going to look utterly ridiculous next to him. Thank heavens he no longer liked me 'cause this moment surely would have killed any desire he had. He was way too gorgeous to ever go for an average-built, poorly-dressed girl like me, especially when he had Izzy to ogle at, like Gabe and the two other men.

But hey, at least no one could claim I was trying to seduce David.

Chapter 7

David

I FULLY EXPECTED THE thief to wear something like Izzy had chosen—and I ignored the petty side of me that was rather eager to see what type of curves Lacy would possess. It didn't really matter since I knew I'd become tongue-tied like I usually did. Josh, at least, had promised to monopolize the thief's time so she wouldn't get a chance to exploit any weaknesses of mine. More reassuring, my lawyers had a warrant ready for her arrest. Once I knew she lied about her lack of swimming ability, I'd make a call and she'd be walking into jail instead of back on the cruise ship and I wouldn't have to deal with her ever again.

But I was not prepared at all to find the thief marching down the dock in an old t-shirt and cut-off jeans that had endured too many wash cycles. She had pulled her hair up into a messy ponytail with enough tendrils escaping to frame her face in an alluring manner.

I swallowed hard and was glad when the instructor launched into his spiel the second Josh and the thief joined the group. Why had she worn that? And why was it far harder for me to resist checking her out than Izzy, who practically had nothing on? The thief must have researched me and deduced what would attract me the best. That had to be the explanation as to why I was hyper-aware of her exact location and kept wanting to brush those tendrils of hair from her face.

I was so glad when the instructor handed out the bright orange life jackets, hoping it would help hide both Izzy and Lacy for me. Except I did not expect the slight tick of resentment as the instructor helped Lacy put on her life jacket, seeming to linger a bit too long with her. Not that I wanted to help her. No, I was not going to get anywhere near her and

I made a point to let everyone else get on first, then made sure I took the side that was opposite the thief.

The boat took off, bouncing slightly as it cut through the waves. I tried my best to keep my eyes on anything but Lacy, but it was like I was a moth and she was a bright light I couldn't avoid. Her posture was also odd. She held onto her seat so hard, her knuckles were turning white, and her eyes stayed on the ocean as if she expected a monster to rise up and eat the boat in one bite. She almost looked exactly like my little sister did before she had managed to overcome her irrational fear of water.

Maybe she really was afraid? If so, forcing her on this trip was wrong.

No, she was a liar. And my experience with Josh told me how easily a liar could pretend whatever emotion was needed. Lacy had probably discovered Jane's near-drowning when she was three. And the thief thought it might endear me to her by acting like my little sister. Yeah, that was it. She might even try to get me to save her. Well, it wouldn't work. I wouldn't fall for her acting charade. She would never get me to believe she was truly freaking out.

Lacy

I was going to die.

The thought kept echoing in my head as I stared out at the blue and green ocean spread out before me. While it had been relaxing to stare at while on the cruise ship, I had been behind a tall railing and the waters had been far below. Now, they were less than ten feet from me and the railing barely hit my shoulders while sitting down. If I stood up, I could fall and nothing would catch me.

The instructor had insisted, when I had confessed I couldn't swim when he put on the life jacket, that I would be okay, and while I had believed him while standing on solid ground, that trust disappeared as fast as the shore did.

I shot a look at Izzy, but she was giggling between Gabe and one of the other guys, obviously not in fear of her life at all. How in the world could she be this relaxed?

Josh sat next to me and I think he tried started a conversation once or twice, but I couldn't open my mouth. I was too afraid I'd start screaming and never stop.

When the boat reached our destination, I remained rooted to my spot as everyone else began hopping into the water, including Josh. He must have given up trying to deal with me. At least I had succeeded at something. I watched as Izzy hesitated at the edge of the boat, but Gabe waited for her in the water, urging her to jump. She did, and she went under immediately with no way to come back up. I caught my breath in a panic, but then she popped up with a laugh. How did she do that? Was there a trick? No one had told me the trick.

What if this was a death trap? And everyone was in on it?

A logical side of me insisted that while Gabe might dislike me a lot, I couldn't see him as the type who would sign on as an accomplice to a murder. And Izzy didn't seem to have enough brains to really understand such a complicated plot. But my suspicious brain was in high gear and I saw death in every direction.

The instructor was by my side, coaxing me to get up. He couldn't be in on the murder, could he? He seemed too nice. But then, David had seemed nice and now he was already in the water, eying me as if daring me to back down.

That spurred me into action and I unlocked my death grip on my seat and followed the instructor's direction toward a ladder where I could ease myself into the water instead of jumping in like the others. That was nice of him. Maybe I could do this.

However, as I grabbed the edge of the boat, I could see into the water and wow, that was deep. The water was clear enough that I could see all the way to the bottom, at least thirty feet below. The deepest water I had ever stepped in was a bathtub, and no amount of lying to myself was going to convince me this was only a bigger bathtub.

"You're going to be okay," the instructor insisted. "Just climb down a few steps. The life jacket won't let you drown."

I wanted to demand the statistics on that. What if one percent of the life jackets didn't work? And with my luck, I would fall under that one percent, no doubt. But I dutifully obeyed and managed to enter the water. It was warm and cool at the same time, lapping at me like a lover. But my dad had been a lover. And he had ruined people that way.

"Just let go now," the instructor said. "You'll be fine, I promise."

My fingers tightened around the ladder, that voice of doom growing louder in my head. How did he know I'd be fine? My father used to tell me that all the time and it had been a lie. Sarah had insisted no one would find out about my past when she convinced me to take the job at her work, and that had ended up as a lie. Everyone lied. Even me. And this instructor was probably doing the same.

My breath started to come quick. I couldn't seem to get enough air. Everything was closing around me. The water was going to swallow me whole.

"I want back up," I whispered. My breath was still hard to find. Why couldn't I breathe right? I was already drowning and I wasn't even in the water yet. "Let me up."

"Are you sure?" the instructor asked. "You haven't tried—"

"Please let me get back up—"

"Lacy," David's voice zapped through my brain. I snapped my head to my right and found David floating effortlessly less than a foot from me. He held a hand out to me. "You're going to be okay. Just grab my hand."

My fingers seemed glued to the ladder. "I can't." I closed my eyes. "Please get me out of here." He probably thought I was some weak female, maybe even a pathetic excuse for an employee, but I didn't care. I just wanted to be back on the boat. No, I wanted to be on land and as far away from the water as possible.

His warm hand covered my frozen fingers. "Remember my sister, Jane? She was terrified of the water, too, but I didn't let her drown. Remember that?"

I did, but that was back when I thought he was nice. I wasn't sure of anything right now. My brain was seeing death in everything.

"You don't have to look," he said, covering my other hand. "Just follow my voice." His tone was so soothing. It reminded me of my mom, during the few times she was sober. She used to cuddle me when I had a bad dream, stroking my hair and murmuring words of comfort. It had made me feel so safe back then.

David's hands peeled my death grip off the ladder, but I still had my feet on the last rung, keeping me out of the hungry waters waiting to eat me.

"Just lean toward me now." His calm voice washed over me.

For a split second, the trust I once had in him re-ignited. And I leaned forward, my feet falling off the ladder.

The water rushed over me, clawing over my shoulders and up my neck. They were going for my face. And then I'd be dead.

I screamed. It erupted out of me like an out-of-control alarm, everything inside me insisting it was life or death if I didn't do something *right now*. I ripped my hands free of David's and slapped my arms against the water, desperate to stay up, but the water wasn't like land. It wasn't holding me up. I couldn't stay up! I was going to die!

Strong arms suddenly wrapped tight around me, locking my arms against my side.

"You are safe," David's voice said in my ear. "There is absolutely no way you can drown. Look, I'm not swimming; you're not swimming, but we're not sinking. You're safe."

Irrational calm hit me like a tidal wave and I stilled, my head dropping forward onto a hard surface as I breathed hard. Encircled in those warm arms, I felt safe. Safer than I had felt in my entire life. It made no sense. I was surrounded by water, but he was right. We were not sinking, but bopping along with every ripple of the water. It was the strangest sensation, as if I weighed no more than ten pounds while I drifted in air. It could even be called peaceful. My head pounded as though a thousand runners were running overhead, though. Oh, wait, that was my heartbeat. And it was slowing down. My lungs could fill with air easier, too. I was going to be okay.

I took a deep breath, then opened my eyes. Only to find myself staring at a chiseled chest of spandex. My head had been resting on his collarbone. And his warm body was wrapped around me tight, the life jackets the only thing keeping us uncomfortably close.

I snapped my head up and found his lips inches from mine. Kissable lips. Why in the world was I thinking that? And why was my breath suddenly hard to catch again?

I needed space. Lots of space from him.

"I-I'm okay," I stuttered, wiggling slightly in the hopes he'd release me. "You can let me go now."

He searched my face for a second. He couldn't possibly still think I was lying, could he?

But he abruptly let go, his arms sliding down my arms, causing goosebumps to run along wherever he touched. Heavens, I was losing my mind to react like this. The guy hated me!

The water suddenly rushed over my shoulders. The fear re-ignited and I immediately reached for something solid, but his hands grabbed my elbows, steadying me. Boy, was this man strong.

"Not so okay?" he asked with a slight grin as if he were teasing me.

"I'm sorry. I'm acting like a total idiot." I should never have agreed to go on this stupid activity. "Just take me back to the boat." I looked around and was shocked to see the boat over ten feet away from me. I instinctively gripped his life jacket and pressed my forehead against his solid chest. A part of me insisted that it was unseemly to cling to my boss like this, but the terrified side of me didn't care. He was more solid than the water around me and I somehow felt a whole lot safer with him than without.

"You've made it this far." I could feel his breath on my ear and it sent shivers up my spine. My body must have lost its mind to be reacting like this. I hoped he only believed it was because of fear and not for very inappropriate reasons.

"Just hang on to me," he continued, "and you'll be fine, all right?"

A part of me wanted to melt into his arms, but the rest of me was exhausted. Swimming was harder than I thought. "What about the instructor?" I muttered.

"I told him to go on ahead. I'll take care of you."

Ugh, now I really wanted to melt into him. He shouldn't be this nice, especially since I had no idea if it was real or not. "Just take me back to the boat. I'm ruining your vacation."

"You're my responsibility," he countered. "I'm the one who encouraged you to come even though I knew you couldn't swim, and I don't need you suing me for emotional damages over this."

My melted heart hardened. That was the reason he was being so nice? So I wouldn't sue him?

"I would never do that," I shot out and tried pushing away from him, but my stupid body refused to obey. My terror of the water was stronger than my anger and my body was not going to move an inch from his solid one, nor did it want his strong hands removed from my elbows. A slightly rational part of my brain tried to insist I wouldn't drown and that I was acting stupid. David had pointed out that neither of us were doing anything remotely to what I would call swimming and yet we continued to stay above the water, the life jackets only half submerged.

"Sorry," he said. "I didn't mean to imply you are the type to do that."

I eyed him. Did that mean he believed me now, or what? I wished I could deduce what he meant but he seemed as confused as me.

"And I'm sorry," he continued. "I did not realize your fear of the water was so strong."

Ah, he believed that, at least! Did that mean I passed the test? Was my stupid inability to swim going to be the thing that saved me? Should I confess that I was not his thief?

Except if he didn't believe me, he would let me go. And I wasn't willing to float by myself in the hungry waters.

"And I'm glad you really are a good swimmer," I said instead.

A slight smile crossed his lips. "I wouldn't call this swimming, but thanks."

"We're not drowning," my stubborn brain insisted on saying. "That must mean we're swimming."

His smile grew into a grin. "You really have no idea what swimming is. Maybe I should teach you."

I shook my head. "Please not now. If I sank, no one would be able to retrieve my body."

Now he laughed. "You're not going to sink with this life jacket tied on to you, okay? But I agree. Now is not a good spot. How about we snorkel instead?"

I looked at my fingers, still wrapped tight around the straps of his life jacket. "I'm not sure I can."

He rubbed a thumb against my elbow. It reminded me of my mother's calming strokes on my hair. "I'll be with you the entire time, all right? I won't let you go until you're ready, okay?"

He was being so nice again. I really liked it when he was like this.

"Okay." The word tumbled out.

Chapter 8

David

Lacy kept a death grip on my hand the entire time I tugged her along. It took a while for me to help her get the snorkeling gear onto her head since I needed both hands and she seemed incapable of floating by herself. But after several attempts to put her head into the water and breathe through the tube, her fear wouldn't let her and we abandoned the process. Whatever type of a swindler she might be, there was no way she could so consistently copy how my sister used to panic whenever she encountered water. Lacy might be a thief, but she hadn't been lying about not knowing how to swim. The panic in her eyes was real.

The memory of my arms around her still lingered in my mind. I couldn't deny how good it felt to be able to calm her down. I had done the same move to my sister plenty of times, but it had never warmed me quite the way it did with Lacy.

But she was a thief. I couldn't forget that. No matter how honest and genuine she seemed, I had to hold onto the fact that she was a skilled swindler with a prison record, according to my lawyers. She was trying to entrap me and I had to be smarter than her.

Still, it was fun showing her the ropes to snorkeling. The way her face lit up as she watched schools of fish swim past. She looked like a kid, with her big eyes staring at everything. It was probably the first time she didn't have that apprehensive look that usually plagued her. She must always be afraid of getting caught in her swindling ways. If so, what an exhausting way to live a life. I wish I could save her from it.

Whoa, where'd that thought come from? I was not getting involved. No way. I didn't care how much I really liked how she grabbed onto me whenever a wave hit her more strongly than she was expecting. It was just a guy thing, like how Josh liked taking girls to haunted houses. It did not mean anything more than that.

Still, I couldn't help feeling disappointed when the instructor signaled for us all to return to the boat. Nor did I like that Josh made sure she sat next to him again instead of by me. I was definitely losing my mind. No matter how many times I reiterated that she was a thief and she was manipulating me to like her, I couldn't stop myself from checking to see if she ever looked in my direction while the boat zoomed back to shore. Unfortunately, she never did. Of course she wouldn't. She was just using me, remember? I was just a pile of billions to steal from.

When we reached the shore, my phone buzzed. My lawyers were waiting on me to move forward with the arrest. I only had today to do it since tomorrow, the cruise ship would enter international waters and it would be four days before we docked at another American port.

I glanced at Lacy as Josh offered to help her out of the boat. She had a look of disgust, a look she seemed to wear constantly whenever Josh was talking to her. I wondered how Josh was taking the obvious dislike. It usually inspired him to try harder—he always loved a challenge. But his whole job here was to find incriminating evidence against her, not get her to like him. That was my job.

What? Where did that thought come from?

I growled mentally at myself. She had me wrapped around her finger this badly and I didn't even know how she had pulled it off! I should send her to jail just to keep myself sane.

"David!" Josh called, interrupting me as I texted my lawyers. "Want to go to lunch with us?"

He had asked her out? I could feel my blood pressure rise slightly and I wanted to shout a firm no, but instead, "Yeah, sure," came out.

Lacy immediately waved her hands. "Neither of you need to come. I'll be fine by myself."

Oh, so she hadn't agreed? My blood pressure dropped.

"Nonsense," Josh said. "David and I know all the haunts around here. We'll make sure you get an authentic experience. Won't we, David?"

I nodded. "We should go for conch fritters."

"Oh, yeah!" Josh said. "I hadn't had one of those in forever. Come on!"

Lacy followed along with us with a stiff gait, her body tense, but the stiffness lessened as we left the ocean behind. She really was afraid of the water, and I felt stupid for doubting her. It had not been fair for me to dump her in the middle of the ocean. It was impressive she had even tried. The girl had spunk.

I shook myself. I couldn't start labeling positive traits she had—she was a thief, and that was the end of it.

Josh secured us a table at one of his favorite local haunts and ordered a bunch of food without bothering to consult with Lacy or me. I didn't mind since I usually liked what Josh liked, but Josh had failed to see if Lacy had any allergies.

"You're not allergic to anything, are you?" I asked as we waited at a table shaded by palm trees, the shoreline within sight, the waves creating a soothing atmosphere. At least, to me. Lacy sat like she was about to face trial, however. I wasn't sure it if was because the ocean was within view or because of us.

A little voice piped up it might be because she knew we knew of her deception but I shooed it away. There was no way she knew about the investigation. Only a few were aware of it and I knew none would divulge the details.

She shook her head. "Not that I know of. What are conch fritters, though?"

"Don't tell her," Josh said with a fake worried look. "She won't eat them then."

She shot Josh a glare. She seemed to do that constantly toward him. "I think I'd rather be the judge of that."

"They're a sea snail," I said and expected her to recoil in distaste like my sisters had done, but she just cocked her head.

"What do they taste like?"

"Ever had lobster?" Josh asked.

She shook her head.

"Clams? Crab? Salmon? Sushi? Anything seafood related?"

She continued to shake her head through Josh's list.

"What on earth do you eat, then?" Josh demanded.

She shrugged. "Peasant food, I guess. Everything you listed is too expensive at the grocery store."

That made me squirm. Sometimes, I forgot the comforts I was used to was a life others dreamed about. I suddenly realized why she was so tense. Josh had just ordered a ton of food and she had no idea what the price was.

Guilt and concern started to spread, but thankfully I remembered she had stolen three million. This was either an act or she had expensive tastes outside of food.

"Well, then," Josh began, "I insist on paying for your meal."

She raised her hands. "No, please, I—"

"I insist," Josh cut in. "David, I'll cover yours, too."

That made me raise an eyebrow, but I knew what he was doing. Lacy couldn't object if I didn't. "You sure?"

"Yep. My treat to you all."

I shrugged. "Okay."

Josh's tactic worked and Lacy offered a lackluster *thank you* in his direction.

The food arrived shortly afterward and, after we pointed out what everything was, Josh dug in with gusto. Lacy, however, was a bit more timid and I watched her, wondering if this really was her first time tasting conch.

Her surprised look and the shudder that went through her definitely looked genuine. She was either telling the truth or she was the best actress I had ever seen. She should work for the CIA if so.

"It's squishy," Lacy said after hastily swallowing the small bite she had taken. "And really weird."

Josh laughed. "You'll learn to love it, trust me."

"It's slightly rubbery," I explained. "A lot of seafood is like that, but conch breaks apart better than, say, octopus."

"Oh, yeah," Josh said with a grin, "Remember when your parents made you all try that takoyaki in Japan? I swear your sister was about to gag to death."

"At least she didn't throw up like your brother did."

Josh laughed. "Oh, yeah. That was like the best thing ever. I don't think he's agreed to try a new food since."

"How long have you two known each other?" Lacy asked.

"Too long," Josh quipped and I gave him a slight rap on the shoulder in protest.

"My father worked for his for a short time," I said. "And they became fast friends. I've been forced to hang out with Josh since."

"Excuse me?" Josh waved a finger. "It's the other way around, buddy." He wiped his mouth for a second. "So, Lacy, what about your parents?"

She had been smiling during our exchange, but the smile died at his question.

"We don't need to talk about my parents."

I raised an eyebrow. She was evading. No doubt wanting to avoid mentioning the scam artist who was her father. I wonder what lie she'd use to cover that fact.

"Are they famous serial killers or something?" Josh teased.

The look of strain on her face increased. "No, it's just... not a fun topic."

Josh leaned forward. "Sounds intriguing."

She shot him a glare. "Fine. My mom drank herself to death and my dad wasn't much better."

It was a practiced line. Probably what she said all the time when asked about her parents. But the bitterness in her voice was sharp and raw and the pain in her eyes was bright. It was too genuine to be a lie. Evasive, yes, but I could tell she held no pride for her parents.

"I told you it's not a fun topic," she stated when neither Josh nor I offered a response.

Josh cleared his throat. "Guess I'm not used to chatting with peasants."

I shot him a look. That hadn't been very nice.

"It's fine," she said. "My parents made their choices. I don't have to follow their examples."

That felt like a dagger directed solely at me. But she had no idea about the investigation. It must be my guilty conscience.

Wait, what guilty conscience? There was no one else who could have stolen those millions. She had to be the thief, no matter what she said about not following after her father.

Josh cleared his throat. "Well—"

"Excuse me?"

We all glanced up to see two nervous girls staring at Josh.

"Are you Josh Covens?"

Chapter 9

Lacy

My jaw dropped as Josh flashed the two nervous girls a dashing smile. "I sure am."

The two girls, not more than twenty years old, erupted into giggles as if they were now twelve-year-olds. "Could we take a picture with you?"

"Sure." Josh stood up. "But let's take it facing the ocean. Make your friends more jealous."

The giggling girls followed him like loyal dogs toward the beach.

I couldn't believe it. I knew Josh tended to act like a celebrity, but I had no idea he actually *was* one.

I leaned toward David. "How famous is Josh?"

He shrugged as if it were no big deal. "Not as famous as he wants to be, so he milks it for all it's worth."

I looked back to Josh, who was now chatting with the awestruck girls. He might be there for a while then. This might be my best moment to talk to David.

I sent up a silent prayer that this might work, then faced David. "There are two things I need to say to you."

He raised his eyebrows as if taken aback. I probably should have started with something less direct, but I didn't really have the time and I hoped blunt honesty would be a plus factor.

"First, I'm so sorry about how I was in the water earlier. Now that I'm on dry land, I can see that I acted completely irrationally." The mere memory embarrassed me and I hoped neither Izzy nor Gabe saw me clinging so hard to David. "I don't normally act like that, I promise. I—"

"It's okay," he cut in. "You panicked. It's a normal response; you don't have to apologize for it. I've seen that reaction dozens of times. My sister, especially, did the same whenever she came into contact with large bodies of water."

"She did?" That made me feel slightly better.

"Yeah, but at least you didn't deck me when I tried to help."

I stared at him, horrified. "Why would she do that?"

"She didn't mean to. She was just trying to grab onto anything solid and whacked me in the process."

"Is-is that why you clamped my arms down?" I asked and tried not to remember how good it felt being held so tight by him.

"Yeah," he said. "People in a panic tend to thrash and I wasn't in the mood to sport another black eye."

Imagining David with a black eye because of his little sister made a laugh dribble out. I immediately covered my mouth. "I'm sorry, that's not funny—"

"Yeah, it is," he said, chuckling. "And I tease my sister about it every chance I get. She's never going to live it down."

I chuckled too. He really loved his sister. It was super cute to see him like that.

"What was the second thing?" he asked with an amused smile.

All joviality died within me. This was the big moment. Oh, I hoped I got it right.

"I know I'm being investigated for stealing money from you," I began.

His face hardened and his body tensed. Not a good sign.

"I didn't do it," I continued. "I know I fit the criteria for the crime, but I swear, I didn't do it. I—"

"How do you know about this?" he cut in, his voice constrained.

I froze, images of Sarah dancing through my head. If I mentioned her, she could get dragged down with me, slapped with a label of being my accomplice.

But if I lied, he would never believe me. Ever.

Yet, Sarah had never gone to jail except to visit her brother. And she had that autoimmune disease. Jail could literally kill her.

"T-things are overheard all the time." It wasn't a lie, but it wasn't a very good truth, either. I could tell by the way he recoiled into his chair. I was messing up my one chance! Why did the truth have to be so complicated?

"So," he began, his cold, brown eyes leveled on me, "I'm to believe that a known convict who's been spewing lies since I met her—"

"That's not true," I shot out. "I lied about my past to get the job, but that was five years ago. In the past twenty-four hours, I have not lied to you. Not once."

"Your name is not Lacy Armstrong."

Of course he'd hit me there, but I had a great comeback. "It has been for the past nine months. I had it legally changed. Your investigators can confirm that."

The anger on his face seemed to crack a little. Progress at last!

"But you have stolen money before," he shot back.

Ouch; my other weak spot. "I grew up with a father that had different ideas of what was right and what wasn't and yes, I helped him. He was my dad. I assumed I could trust him. But landing in juvenile jail woke me up."

He seemed surprised by that. "Juvenile?"

Kevin or whoever had informed him must have forgotten to include that detail. "I was sixteen when my dad got busted. I was an accomplice, so they only gave me two years since I was young. My dad got twenty."

He fell silent for a moment and I could see confusion in his eyes. This might actually work.

But that hope died with his next words. "So you just expect me to believe all this without any proof?"

Yes, I wanted to shout, but I knew it would do no good.

"Honestly?" I said instead. "No. I don't expect you to believe me. I have a record and I've lied in the past. It's a position I can't change. But I'm innocent and I don't have the three million I supposedly stole to hire a good lawyer to fight against you. I wasted all my money just trying to get my fake name to be real so I didn't have to lie anymore. It was going to be a new start for me where I could hold my head up high and not be afraid of my past. All I'm asking is for you to at least give me a chance. Find the proof first, then charge me. Don't assume I'm guilty because I happened to be in the wrong place at the wrong time with a past record."

I held my breath as he searched my face.

But Josh ruined the moment by returning to the table. "Hey all, what did I miss?"

The anger returned to David's face. "Lacy was just leaving."

Ouch, that hurt. But I tried to keep the dismay off my face. "Thank you for your time," I said as I rose. "And thanks, Josh, for the meal." I then walked away, hoping I didn't look like how I felt inside, ready to crumble at the first touch. I had a sinking feeling that I had ruined my last chance for freedom.

David

"What was that about?" Josh asked, glaring down at me as if I was the problem and not Lacy.

"She knows."

"Knows what?"

"About the stolen millions."

Josh sat down at once. "She confessed?"

I wished she had. "She's insisting she's innocent."

"But how did she know about the theft?"

"She wouldn't tell me." That irked the most. For someone who insisted she was now honest, she sure didn't give a lot of honest answers. And now I couldn't help feeling she had an accomplice, which meant I had two employees stealing from me. My investigators needed to broaden their search.

"So, she's just hoping you'll believe she's innocent?" Josh asked.

I nodded, my eyes on Lacy's retreating form. She was heading to the ship, no doubt. I determined to have officers waiting for her there.

Josh leaned back against his chair. "You should believe her."

I snapped my eyes to him in shock. "What? Why?"

"'Cause she's a terrible liar. I've been chatting with her for the past couple of hours. When she's comfortable with an answer, she stares right at you and delivers it very bluntly. When she's not, her answer is clumsily evasive and her whole body gives away that she's uncomfortable."

I had noticed that as well. "It could be an act—"

"Now you're sounding paranoid."

"No, I'm pushing away emotion and sticking to the facts—"

Josh groaned. "Now you're doing your dad thing. I hated it when he did that."

I glared at him. "It's the best way to make decisions. Emotions blind you into doing stupid things."

Josh raised an eyebrow. "Oh, yeah? Then, by your so-called facts, you should have cut me as a friend years ago."

I looked away. "That's not the same thing—"

"Your dad doesn't agree."

I looked away. My family had never understood why I maintained Josh's friendship. His partying and womanizing ways were a PR nightmare for his own family. But despite Josh's problems, I knew he was loyal and reliable in his own way. And I could be my grumpy self around him and he wouldn't get upset about it. In fact, he usually got me out of those moods.

But this problem was not about our friendship. I had a thief who needed to be caught.

I rubbed my face. "I don't like the idea that someone else could have done it."

"So you'd rather blame a girl?"

I dropped my hand to glare at him. "Or maybe you just want to believe in her because she *is* a girl."

"She's too blunt for my taste. And it's that bluntness that makes me believe her." Josh repositioned his chair so it faced mine. "Now, who else could have done it?"

I rubbed my face again. "She has two co-workers, but they wouldn't have had access to her accounts without her helping them." That might be where the accomplice had come in. Though I didn't understand why she would resort to having one since then it would mean she had to share. And thieves weren't known for their sharing.

"What about the employees on this cruise? Any of them had access?"

"Most of them don't. They're in different branches. But, let's see, Gabe—"

"Oh, the one with Izzy?" Josh asked.

"Yeah."

He rubbed his hands together. "I'll start questioning him, then."

I leveled a stare at him. "No."

He looked up in surprise. "Why not?"

"'Cause all you're going to do is spend your time with Izzy, and she works in a completely different department and has no clearance in this matter."

Josh wagged his finger at me. "I'll have you know that women can be an impressive well of knowledge about the guy they're dating or have dated."

"But Gabe is one of my best employees and he's a widower with three teenage kids. I don't need you messing up the first promising relationship he's had since his wife died."

"But I though inter-office relationships are bad."

"That was my dad's rule. I've relaxed it. As long as they follow the protocols my lawyers put in place, it is allowed."

"But when the relationship goes south, you'll have a PR nightmare since one can start accusing the other of sexual harassment. Now, if I come in—"

"They don't work in the same department and Gabe's made sure he doesn't oversee anything she's involved in *and* he made sure the HR department is aware of the situation. He has followed the protocols, so leave Izzy alone."

"Fine," Josh sighed. "I'll stick with the boring Gabe. But you can't blame me if it so happens that I'm found chatting with Izzy. It would be rude to just ignore her."

I gave him a warning glare. "If they end up breaking up, I'll be blaming you."

"Then I'll make sure they get a notarized note saying it wasn't me."

I struggled not to smile at that. "Come on. We should head back."

While Josh paid for the meal, I pulled out my phone, my half-written text to arrest Lacy still waiting to be finished. I eyed it for a long moment, then replaced it by asking them to hold off until the cruise was finished. Next, I tapped out an email to my investigators, asking them to widen their net and not focus so much on Lacy unless they found absolute proof she had committed the crime.

I wasn't going to believe Lacy was innocent, but she had been right that it was cruel to not give her the benefit of the doubt at least.

Chapter 10

Lacy

"IF YOU HEAR A lot of sudden noise," I said, "it's because I'm getting arrested."

"He didn't believe you?" Sarah asked. Since I was still technically in the United States, I had called her up to give her an update before I lost service.

"No, and I think I made it worse." I eyed the door to my cabin, fully expecting armed officers to be bursting through at any moment. "He wanted to know how I knew about the theft."

Sarah gasped. "You told him about me?"

"No."

"You lied?"

"Technically, no. I gave a half-truth but it wasn't very convincing." I sighed. "Sarah, what are you going to do?"

"Me? What are *you* going to do?"

"Go to jail, obviously, but I've been there before. I know that life already. But what about you? With your disease—"

"No, don't waste time worrying about me. You can still salvage this. I mean, it's late for you right now, isn't it? Shouldn't the ship be leaving the dock soon?"

I glanced out the small, round window. To my surprise, the shoreline was receding. "I think we've left."

"Then that's a good sign! You're not going to be arrested!"

"Yet," I muttered.

"Ha, and you always insist I'm the pessimistic one," she teased.

That made me smile. "Well, you always countered that you were just being practical. I'm following your example now."

"I do a better job than that."

I laughed. "Well, you're not the one who messed everything up today."

"Hey, you're still free, aren't you? And you got to talk to David. Is he as handsome as I remember?"

"I am not going to comment on the attraction level of the man who is planning on sending me to jail," I retorted. I hadn't told her anything about the boat ride or how David had come to my rescue. Nor did I mention he possibly initially liked me before he realized who I was. Sarah would read too much into it. She'd always been the romantic one even though both of us avoided dating. I always hoped she'd find someone but neither of us had good prospects. Besides, stress triggered her disease and while she might dream about dashingly handsome men, she could barely talk to them.

"Well," she continued, "at least you're on a Caribbean cruise."

I could hear the envy in her voice. She'd never managed to win a spot for the company retreat. Even though she had worked longer at our company than me, she didn't have the talent for numbers that I did and so while I got promoted, she had been left behind.

"Then I'll enjoy this for the both of us," I said.

"That's the spirit!"

We switched to easier topics, then bid goodbyes before I headed off to bed. But I didn't sleep well. Nightmares of officers barging into my cabin and dragging me out woke me up in a panic at least three times.

I gave up and stared out my window, watching the dark sea slowly light up with hues of pinks and reds as the sun rose. I debated headed up onto the deck, but I wasn't sure I wanted to hear the ocean. The experience yesterday had left a searing mark.

A speck began to grow in the distance until an island grew into form, sporting long, white beaches all over the place. With all the stress from yesterday, I never really got a chance to enjoy Key West. But today would be different. Grand Turk was officially outside of the United States and nothing was going to ruin my first taste of an international country.

I donned shorts and a light blouse along with a hat and shoes geared for lots of walking. I knew most people wouldn't leave the cruise center, but since all the activities listed seemed to either involve water or shopping, I wanted to escape and explore the actual island itself.

Hoping to not run into David or Josh, I was first in line when the breakfast buffet opened and I managed to eat and be in the departure line without seeing either. I was still badly shaken from the failure of convincing David I was innocent and, adding the humiliating snorkeling experience and the fear of my stupid past, I just wanted to relax—and that meant being by myself.

Despite being armed with a map, I got turned around in the cruise center area and struggled to find the exit. My sense of direction had never been stellar and now I was about to navigate a foreign island by myself? Maybe this wasn't such a good idea...

No, I could do this. I just needed to find someone who could help me. Unfortunately, I found the one couple I didn't want to meet.

"Lacy!" Izzy cried as she dragged Gabe over to me, his face stating very loudly that he had a very different opinion of this budding friendship between me and Izzy. I wasn't so sure of it myself, but I couldn't deny it was nice to see someone happy to see me. That certainly wasn't the case with David.

"I'm so glad you spotted us!" Izzy continued. "We never got a chance to chat after the snorkeling adventure."

"You should go for another one," Gabe said with a smirk.

"Oh, yes!" Izzy cried. "They say you can snorkel right off the beaches here. We should do it together!"

I grimaced. "I have other plans."

"Are you going shopping? Gabe here," Izzy poked his arm, "refuses to spend hours shopping. Can you imagine? Who doesn't shop when they travel?"

That would be me, but then, I was living on credit card debt as it was. Izzy shouldn't have enough money for endless spending, either—her job was lower than mine. Gabe had a cushy senior manager job, but he still had kids to raise, so I could understand his desire to not blow through his savings.

"If you want to shop, babe," Gabe said, "go right ahead."

She shrieked. "Really?"

"Just don't take me with you." He handed her his credit card and she did a little dance.

I shifted my weight, not entirely sure that was very wise of Gabe to do. My mother had been dangerous when armed with credit cards.

Izzy grabbed my arm. "Let's go shopping!"

"No," Gabe said, intervening. "She had other plans."

"But I can't shop alone!"

"I don't really like to shop," I said.

Izzy stared at me as if I had shattered all her dreams. "How can you function?"

Gabe wrapped an arm around her shoulders. "Let her do her thing, Izzy." He steered her away toward a nearby shop, probably in the hopes of both distracting her and cheering her up.

"Next time, Lacy!" Izzy called over her shoulder, then rushed into the store to shop until she dropped, no doubt.

I shook my head over the two. That was not a relationship I would enjoy being in. Dating someone who had a lot more money than me would be unsettling. I'd always feel like I was in debt to him.

Not that I'd ever find a rich guy to be interested in me.

Well, a voice piped up in my head, *David had shown interest.*

Yeah, I shot back, *but then he found out about my past.*

Not wanting my brain to respond, I focused on the map and managed to locate the exit at last. A row of taxis waited and, while I had no intention of using them, some of the drivers were kind of enough to make sure I walked in the correct direction toward the main town.

With their approval, I set off. I only had about four hours before I had to be back at the cruise center, so that would only give me about two hours in the town. I would have loved to explore further and get up to a lighthouse at the north end of the island, but I had to be content with the little available to me. Maybe next time, when I was loaded with cash and had no worries in the world, I would get a chauffeur and have them take me on a long tour. Ha, like that was ever going to happen. But it was nice to dream about.

David

My windows faced the ocean this time, so I opened the balcony door, propped up my feet against one chair, and worked on my laptop. The noise from the crowds debarking, the ocean hitting the crowded beaches, and the squawking seagulls would be my new soundtrack as I worked.

The opening of the guest bathroom door added to the music, and Josh's stomping feet provided a much-needed bass. But then Josh ruined it by opening his mouth.

"What are you doing?"

I glanced over at him. He stood half-naked with one towel wrapped around his waist while he used a second towel to dry his blond locks.

"Working," I said.

"Exactly, and we agreed you can't work in here."

"You have a whole island to woo some girl. You don't need this space."

"But you need the vacation," Josh shot back.

"I did this cruise too many times while growing up. I'd rather work."

Josh leaned against the window, blocking my view. "How long have you ever been without your precious laptop?"

I ignored him and focused on the email I was trying to finish.

"I bet you couldn't last one hour without it."

"Josh, I'm not a trust-fund kid. I have a company to run and a thief to catch. Aren't you supposed to be trailing Gabe today, anyway?"

Josh groaned. "They left super early this morning."

"I would not consider nine in the morning to be super early."

"It is in my book," Josh said. "There should be a law against anything happening before ten."

"I've been up since six." I had never done well with the whole sleeping-in notion. Staying in bed that long was boring.

"So you should have finished everything by now. So, out!"

"No."

"How about this, then. You go out for two hours and talk to one girl. Just one girl. Do that, and then I'll let you stay in here all day tomorrow without bothering you."

I eyed him. "Why is a girl in this?"

"Because it's painful watching you talk to a girl. You need the practice. Now, go and do that or I'll stay here and annoy you." He began rapping on the window as if it were a drum.

I groaned. "Why are you doing this? I have to work!"

"I'm trying to stop you from turning into your dad. He's had, what, three heart attacks already."

I sank into my chair. "He's only had two."

"And you're going to end up exactly like him. All work, no play, and dead before you reach sixty if you keep this up."

I glared at my laptop, well aware he was right. It was the reason I had fought so hard to take over the company early from my father. I wanted him to enjoy life before the stress killed him. But I wasn't sure how to destress, myself. I had followed in my father's footsteps, and work was the easiest thing to do.

"I already got a car reserved," Josh continued. "It's in my name but I'll call and get it changed into yours."

"I'm not taking a limo," I muttered.

"Then it's your lucky day. It's a boring, regular sedan. You even have to drive it all by yourself."

I looked up, impressed, until he added, "They had no limos available."

I laughed. "I knew it."

"Hey, so I like living it up. What's wrong with that?"

"The attention," I grumbled as I packed my laptop into my bag.

Josh grabbed the bag. "You can't take that with you. It's supposed to be a vacation!"

I eyed him. "If I don't take it, then I don't have to talk to a girl."

We stared at each other for a full minute, then Josh released my bag. "Fine. But it better be a girl your age and not a store clerk! I'll be expecting pictures as proof!"

"Yeah, right," I muttered as I headed out, my bag tucked under my arm. I'd talk to some girl just to get Josh off my back, but pictures were only going to happen if the sky fell down.

Ten minutes later, I was in the sedan, but I sat there for a full two minutes, wondering what to do. I'd been on this island too many times to need to explore it. And while I could lounge on a beach, the glare of the sun made it hard to work on a laptop. Not to mention the sand could ruin the keyboard. A restaurant would be more enjoyable and I might have more selection of which girl to attempt a conversation with. Or maybe I'd get lucky and a girl would approach me for directions or something. Josh would insist it didn't count, but I'd make sure it did.

Remembering which side of the road I needed to be on, I headed for the main town. Halfway there, however, I spotted a woman walking alongside the road. I grinned as an idea sprouted. Offering the woman a ride would count as talking to her and since it was only another two minutes to the town, the whole thing would be painless. That would get me off the hook with Josh and then I could hole up somewhere and work in peace.

I slowed down and rolled down the window, then lost all air in my lungs.

It was Lacy.

The idea to abruptly speed away sprung to mind, but that would be rude. She was already looking at me in surprise. So much for this being painless.

"Want a ride?" I asked.

The look on her face was not filled with relief or joy. "No thanks. I'm good."

Why was she refusing? Now she was making me look ridiculous. "It's another mile from here. I'll save you twenty minutes."

She folded her arms. "I don't know what you're doing, but for someone who is accusing me of stealing three million, offering a ride seems like a slap to the face. So, thanks, but no thanks. I'd rather walk."

Why did she have to make such a good point? Now I looked like the bad guy. "I asked my investigators to widen their search."

Her defiant stance wilted, the hope in her eyes hurting me more than her early argument. "Y-you did? So you believe me?"

I stared out at the road for a second. "You claim you like honesty, right?"

"Yes." There was no hesitation in that response.

I blew out my breath for a second. "You fit the criteria for the crime perfectly, but since there's no smoking gun—yet—I agree it's not fair to assume you did it without solid evidence. So I'm giving you the benefit of the doubt. For now."

The hope died in her eyes. "So you don't believe me."

"I don't know what to believe," I shot back. "I'm waiting for solid evidence."

"And is this offer of a ride some sort of a test?"

"No," I muttered, wishing I had never had slowed down. I was going to curse Josh the second I saw him again. "I was just being nice."

She arched an eyebrow and folded her arms again. "To a girl you want to throw in jail for a crime she didn't commit? In my book, that's cruel, not nice."

Another excellent point. Why did she have to be so stubborn and smart? "Look, I didn't know it was you when I slowed down, but now it's really awkward fighting with you. Just get in and let me drive you somewhere and we can be done, okay? You can get in the backseat and treat me like a chauffeur or something. I don't care. Just get in so we can both stop looking like fools."

She cocked her head. "You're offering to be my chauffeur?"

"Sure," I muttered. "Just get in."

A glint of amusement sprang into her eyes. I wasn't sure what that meant, but she climbed into the backseat and that was all that I cared about. This day had gone from bad to worse. I needed to stop letting Josh bully me into being sociable. It always ended in failure.

"To the lighthouse, chauffeur," Lacy announced from behind me.

I turned toward her in surprise. "That's all the way at the top of the island."

She folded her arms again. "You said you'd take me anywhere. Well, that's where I want to go."

"You were planning on *walking* all the way there?" That would have taken her two to three hours just to get there. She would never have made it back to the ship on time.

"I don't believe a chauffeur is supposed to ask questions."

Lacy wasn't just a thief. She was a smart-aleck, conniving woman.

"This is not helping your case," I stated as I put the car into gear.

"You're the one that insisted I had to get into your car," she shot back. "Technically, I'm being stupid getting in since you could be a kidnapper that is going to steal all my money."

I snorted at the absurd idea. "Maybe if you were carrying that three million on you."

"Right along with the five million I stole from Josh. Or is he faking being rich and mooching off you?"

"I'm pretty sure swindlers research this type of stuff," I countered.

"Right, sorry. I must have missed that class during swindler school."

I had to bite back a chuckle. "A swindler school sounds like the type to scam you out of a proper education."

I expected another snappy response. Instead, I got a bitter: "Yeah, they did."

I checked the rearview mirror and though her face was in profile to me as she glared out the window, pain emanated from it. She looked broken.

She had claimed to be in jail by the time she was sixteen because she helped her dad, didn't she? At that same age, I was also helping my father, though our business was legit.

But, what if it hadn't been?

The image of my father, standing with his hands clasped behind his back, gazing out of his corner office and reveling over the company he had built, had always inspired me. But if I had learned that he had somehow been involved in some shady business, how would I have taken the news?

It would have shattered me.

I eyed her in the rearview mirror again. If what she claimed was true, then she had had a very hard life. And I was only making it harder.

The idea did not sit well with me.

"Tell me about your dad," I asked.

Chapter 11

Lacy

I SNAPPED MY EYES toward David's head over the driver's seat. Why was he asking about that?

"I don't like talking about my dad."

"Do you talk to him often?" David asked.

That sounded like a baited question. He might claim he was giving me the benefit of the doubt, but his actions didn't seem to agree. "I'll be happy to hand over my phone records to prove I have no contact with my dad."

"No, that's not—" David blew out his breath, looking flustered. "I'm just... trying to understand you."

I glared out the window, torn. He wanted to understand me? Well, I wanted to understand him first. David could be so nice, but then he'd change at the drop of a hat and rip everything apart. I would rather he stayed mean. I knew how to deal with those types of people.

He cleared his throat. "You said you went to jail when you were sixteen, right?"

Why was he bringing this up? "Yes."

"Did you have any idea that what you were doing with your dad was wrong?"

There was no safe answer to that. "I feel like I should have a lawyer present."

His eyes found mine in the rearview mirror for a second. "I'm not trying to interrogate you."

I scoffed. "You *want* me to be guilty. That means everything I say can be used against me." I wasn't going to fall for a trap like my dad did.

David was silent for a moment. "I'm giving you the benefit of the doubt that you're innocent. I think it's fair to ask you to give me the benefit of the doubt that I'm not trying to frame you."

I stewed on that for a second. "That would be fair except for the fact that the balance of power is entirely on your side."

"What do you mean?"

"For starters, I'm in your car. It could be bugged."

"It's a rental—"

"Second, if you're wrong, you can still win and throw me in jail. If I'm wrong, you win again and throw me in jail. And third, you're my boss. Even if I can prove myself innocent, you can fire me out of spite. So, no, I'm not going to give you an inch when you can easily take a mile and run me over for the fun of it."

He was silent for so long, I figured I'd messed up big time and was going to get fired. This whole honesty thing wasn't really working out for me these days. When he pulled into the parking lot of the lighthouse and turned to face me, I braced for his anger.

"First," he began, "I would never fire you out of spite."

I arched an eyebrow, not in the least reassured.

"Second, you're right. You're not in a good position here."

I lowered my eyebrows. I hadn't expected that.

"Third, I wanted you to be guilty because out of all the possible culprits, you were the easiest and least painful to get rid of."

"Gee, thanks," I muttered.

"But now you're making me care about you and so I don't know what to do."

My mouth dropped open. Did he just say—

He rubbed his face, a grimace marring his mouth. I had a feeling he regretted what he had just said. Did that mean he meant it?

"Get out," he said.

Nope, he did not mean it.

I shoved the car door open, then barely resisted slamming it shut. I stomped to the front of the car only to be shocked to find him rounding the car as well.

I immediately backed up, nervous. "What are you doing?"

"You've never been here. I'll give you a tour."

"Why?"

He threw up his hands. "I don't know. You frustrate me like no one else but your pain seems genuine and raw and I hate the idea that I might be making your life worse if I'm wrong and you're not the thief."

He glowered at the rock-strewn ground and looked so flustered and confused that my heart went out to him. Maybe he really was a nice guy and I was wrecking his perfect world of black and white. And I would never admit to it, but I would love a free tour.

"Okay, some ground rules," I said. "For this tour, you assume I'm innocent and I'll assume you're not trying to ruin me. And absolutely no asking about my past or anything that makes me uncomfortable." I held out my hand to him. "Deal?"

He eyed my hand for a second. "Will you tell me it's uncomfortable instead of evading?"

"I can do that."

"Then it's a deal." He gave my hand a firm shake.

David

I regretted the handshake the second my hand left hers because it dawned on me that all the questions I wanted to ask were now in the forbidden zone. How was I supposed to fill the awkward silence between us?

Oh, right. The lighthouse tour.

I directed her toward the old building and recited the relatively few facts I knew about it. But when she asked a dozen more, I realized I was woefully unprepared to do a tour.

"I don't think I make a good tour guide," I said as I resorted to looking up the answers on my phone.

"Missed some class during tour school, I see?" She delivered it in a deadpan voice, but I caught the impish light in her eyes.

I fought back a laugh. "Don't tell my family. I'm supposed to be perfect."

"Really, perfect?" The scoff was obvious in her voice.

I shrugged. "Comes with being the oldest, I guess."

"I thought the only child was supposed to be perfect."

"No, that would be spoiled rotten."

I expected her to smile, but pain ricocheted across her face and she looked away. Anything about her growing up days seemed to touch a raw nerve. Questions burned on my tongue, but I had a feeling it would be breaking the deal—and I didn't break deals.

Since I had nothing new to add to the lighthouse, we walked closer to the beach.

"What is something about you that would not make you uncomfortable to talk about?" I ventured.

She seemed surprised by the question. "Uh, well, I made some macros that impressed my old boss so much, he promoted me."

I raised my eyebrows. "Are you bragging?"

The openness she had suddenly shut down. "Never mind. I'm not comfortable talking about it anymore."

I mentally kicked myself. "Sorry. I'm actually really good at making conversations uncomfortable. It's a curse of mine where I'm always eating my own foot."

A ghost of a smile touched her lips. "Well, to be honest, I prefer your awkwardness."

I stared at her for a second. "Y-you do? But, I make an idiot of myself."

She shrugged. "It's cute." Her eyes suddenly went wide. "I-I mean, in a non-attractive cute—"

I burst out laughing. "Now you're sounding as bad as I do."

"Your curse is infectious, apparently," she said with a slight tone of bitterness, but the smile on her face told me she was teasing.

"So, now that we've established we're both bad at making un-awkward conversation, can we restart?"

She cocked her head. "How far back? Should we re-introduce ourselves?"

I groaned. "You saying I've been that bad since the very beginning?"

"Sorry, no, I was just trying to establish your meaning."

I rubbed my temples. "I think we officially ruined our re-start."

She laughed. "Yeah, I think we did."

"How about you just tell me about these macros you're so proud about?"

"Well, it's kind of hard to explain without a computer, but basically..." She launched into a description of what one of the macros could do.

"Wait a minute," I said. "I use these macros."

"You do?"

"Yeah, they're brilliant."

She completely lit up, like I had handed her a medal. Wow, she was pretty like that.

"Really?" she breathed.

I switched my gaze to the ocean, fighting to catch my breath. I was suddenly quite warm. It took me a second to remember what the conversation was about. "Yeah, saved me an hour of work a day." I paused. "But Sam, your old boss, when he sent them to me, he didn't say you made them."

The light in her died like a Christmas tree being snuffed out. "You don't think I made them."

"No, that's not what I meant." I blew out my breath. "I just don't like the idea that someone claimed someone else's work. I gave him a bonus for those macros." The very thought that I might have rewarded the wrong person made my skin crawl. I didn't like being deceived.

I faced her. "Don't take this wrong, but can you prove you made them? I trust Sam, but I also want to trust you. This makes this decision difficult. I just... want some proof. I don't like acting on emotion."

She nodded. "I can provide proof. I'd been using them for a year before I showcased them, so they're all over my old spreadsheets. They've been filed; I'm sure you can bring them up."

I kicked the sand. Sam had *lied* to me. But something was wrong in Lacy's statement. "Why did you wait a year?"

She hunched her shoulders and stared at the ground. I recognized that stance. She did that when she was uncomfortable with a question. I had made a deal not ask such questions, but this couldn't count. She was accusing someone else of lying. I needed the truth.

"Please don't avoid the question," I said. "I need the answer."

She kept her eyes on the ground. "I wasn't ready then."

"Ready for what?"

She raised her head, a defiant light in her eyes. "For this. The questions. The spotlight. People wanting to get to know me more. You know my past. I was scared if I made too many waves, people would start poking and they'd find my web of lies."

That... actually made some sense. "What made you feel like you were ready now?"

"My new name." She started walking along the beach again. "It felt good knowing I didn't have to be ashamed of that anymore." She abruptly stopped, alarm crossing her face. "You know, if I hadn't shared those macros, I would not have been promoted. And if I hadn't been promoted, then I wouldn't have had access to those accounts."

I could see where she was going. "Which means no one could have blamed you for stealing the money," I finished for her.

She covered her face. "I knew I shouldn't have shared them. So stupid!"

"Hey." I put a hand on her back. She looked so distraught, I wanted to somehow ease her pain. But pulling her into a comforting hug seemed awkward. "For what it's worth, I'm glad you shared them. I use them all the time."

A weak laugh dribbled out of her and she seemed to sway, as if wanting to lean against me. A good chunk of me would be totally fine with that result. I've been wanting her in my arms for a while.

Whoa, I should not be thinking like that.

A more innocent thought popped up. "How many other macros are you keeping in hiding?"

"You still don't think I made them?" she muttered through her fingers.

"No, I just... I guess I'm being selfish and was hoping you could make more for some of my routine tasks."

"No." There was a lot of vehemence behind that one word.

I pulled my hand away. "Sorry. I was just trying to make you feel better."

"No, that's not—" Lacy uncovered her face. "You're offering me access to your spreadsheets, which means if something else gets stolen, you'll be able to blame me for that, too."

As always, she made an excellent point. "How about I give you some spreadsheets from several years ago? That way, the data is old and irrelevant, but the tasks should be about the same."

She eyed me as if trying to decide whether to trust me. It was weird to think she saw me as the bad guy in all of this. Then again, if I was in her shoes and I was innocent, I *would* be the bad guy.

It was not a comfortable thought.

"How about," she began, "you tell me what your routine tasks generally do and I'll make up numbers in a new spreadsheet and go with that?"

"Deal. My laptop is in the car."

"You want them right now?"

"Why not?" I was supposed to be working anyway. Oh, wait, she was supposed to be on vacation. "How about I treat you to lunch? Best local place on the island with a great view in exchange for a few macros?"

She eyed him for a second. "Can you throw in the scenic route to this place?"

I laughed. She certainly had a knack for bargaining. "Yeah, I'll throw that in, too."

She smiled, her body relaxing. "Then I agree."

Chapter 12

Lacy

DAVID HADN'T BEEN LYING. The restaurant had a great view and the food was even better. But none of that compared to the praise he kept heaping on me.

"This is amazing!" he said for the third time when I whipped up another macro to simplify a task he had described. I was sure I was beet red and grinning like an idiot, but I asked for another challenge. It felt so good being noticed for something I was good at—something *legal* I was good at. I wanted this to never end.

"You're like a magician," David said as I worked on his next request. "How'd you get so good at this?"

I ducked my head. "I've always been good at numbers and computers."

"There's got to be more to the story than that."

I froze for a second—the answer would require talking about my parents. But he already knew about them. It was such a strange thought. I didn't have to be afraid.

"My mom, she, uh, wasn't good with numbers, so I helped her out."

He propped an elbow on the table and shot me a piercing look. "That's evasive. Our deal was for you to tell me if you didn't like the question, not to evade it."

"Oh, sorry. I didn't mean—I think it must be a habit. I... have a hard time talking about my parents."

His gaze softened. "Because of the unhappy ending?"

"Kind of? Honestly, I'm... I'm ashamed of them. You already know about my dad. As for my mom, well, her favorite places were either in a gambling joint or a bar. Bonus points if they were combined."

I waited for him to recoil in disgust, but he didn't move, his gaze unwavering. To think, this rich, hot guy really wanted to hear about my lame life? I had to be dreaming. No way this was going to end right.

I cleared my throat when I realized he was still waiting for me to finish. "My mom dragged me along when I was young and I'd sit at her feet and try to keep myself entertained, so I started counting. I'd count the machines, the people, the sounds, the pings, how many people were winning, how many were losing, the hours in between and on and on. Then my dad got me this old clunker of a laptop and I started lugging that around and fiddling with the spreadsheets to keep track of all my silly calculations. When I discovered macros, it was like a whole new world opened up. I'd make ones up just to see what would happen. So, yeah, been basically been doing this since I was a kid."

His gaze had slowly morphed into an annoyed one as I talked. I knew my past was going to ruin this.

"I can't believe," David began, "that Sam lied and took credit for your skills."

Oh. So, he wasn't mad about my past. Weird.

"I think what Sam did is my fault, actually," I said.

He shot me a look. "Why?"

"He wanted to make a big deal about it but all the attention started to scare me. So I told him I didn't want a bunch of people to know about it. I insisted I only made the macros to help out the team and that I didn't want credit for it. So he just gave me a promotion and a bonus..." I trailed off. "You know what, I think he gave me the bonus you gave him."

"You sure?" David asked.

"It had been a really big bonus." I was able to pay off several credit cards with it. Which meant I had the money to later buy the flirty dress that I wished I had worn today.

No, I did not wish that. David was my boss, this wasn't a date, and he still didn't trust me.

David rubbed his face. "Well, that makes me feel better. He was just respecting your wishes. But..." He blew out his breath. "This is just frustrating."

"What is?"

"Your abilities should not be hidden as some clerk in one of my branch's accounting departments. You should be doing tech support at the headquarters."

My eyes widened. "A-are you promoting me?"

"I would in a heartbeat except for, well..."

Oh, yeah. The three million question.

I sighed. "I wish I could convince you I'm innocent."

He sighed as well. "I wish I could believe you, but everyone who has access to pull off that theft is someone I trust."

"Except me."

"At first, yes, but, you're growing on me."

The relief and happiness bursting from that statement insisted I should hug him, but I resisted and managed a small smile of thanks instead.

"But," he continued, "that means—"

"That someone you trust is lying to you." I knew that feeling. It had nearly destroyed me when I realized who my father really was. "I'm sorry. That's not a good position to be in."

"Tell me about it," he muttered. "And I need to make a decision before this cruise ends."

"Why?"

He was silent for a moment. "My dad. I, uh, forced him to retire due to his growing health problems, but I know he's chomping at the bit to take over again if I can't show that I can handle this. If he finds out that not only did I fail to catch losing millions, but I don't even know who did it..." He trailed off with an unintelligible mutter, but the frustration on his face was easy to read.

I bit my lip for a second. "Could I know which accounts, exactly, were stolen from?"

He shot a wary glance at me. So much for his growing trust. "Why?"

"I know you have investigators on the case, but I'm good with numbers and computers, too. Maybe I could help to figure out who did it."

He eyed me as if weighing a bunch of options in his head. I held his gaze, refusing to back down.

His phone abruptly buzzed, breaking his concentration. He glanced at it, then abruptly stood. "We're going to miss the ship."

I shot to my feet, checking my own phone for the time. We only had minutes before we missed the deadline. "Will they leave without us?" I didn't have the money to try to fly home from this island. I didn't even have money to find a hotel to spend the night. I had a credit card for emergencies I could use, but I really didn't want to rack another couple of thousand of dollars in debt again.

"Don't worry about it." David dropped several large bills onto the table and I had to bite back a gasp. That was how much this meal had cost? That was more than I spent for a month on groceries!

"Are you saying," I continued as we rushed to the car, "they'd hold the ship for you?" I could see them doing that.

"They might, but if not, I'll just fly us to the next island." He made it sound like it would be a minor hindrance instead of the world-shattering dilemma it would be for me. Sometimes, I forgot how rich this man was.

David

Josh was waiting for me in the cabin and I remembered with a jolt the sole reason I had gone out in the first place.

"You were out all four hours!" Josh began. "I'd clap but I have a sneaky suspicion the only girl you talked to was the server to refill your drink."

"The server was male." I headed for my usual spot at the table next to the windows. The ship was already starting to move. Lacy and I had been late but the ship had waited for us after all, no doubt on account of me. I had parted from Lacy to head for the bridge to apologize directly to the captain, but I was more disturbed by the fact that I found myself wishing I had lingered a little longer with Lacy.

Yet, her question for more details of the theft bothered me. A lot.

Josh joined me at the table and propped his elbows on the table. "I take it this grumpiness means you did not speak to a girl?"

"No, I did."

Seeing the surprise on Josh's face made me feel slightly better.

"For how long?" Josh demanded.

"Pretty much the whole time I was out."

His jaw dropped. "David Wellington, I do not believe you. I want proof."

"I don't have it." I pulled out my laptop.

"Did you at least get her name? Is she from this cruise or another one? Or a native?"

"I know the answer to all of those but I'm not divulging them."

"What? Why not?"

"Because I don't need your opinion on this." I put my laptop on my lap, then turned away from him and faced the big windows. Though I no longer could see Josh, I could hear the eager glee in his laugh.

"You like her!"

That was not something I wanted to admit.

"She has to be on this ship or you wouldn't be acting like this."

I hunkered lower into my chair.

"I shall have to stalk you tomorrow to see who this girl is."

"I won't be seeing her," I shot back. "I did what you asked, so I get to work in here tomorrow." The whole thing with Lacy was awkward. She was my employee, for one, and while I was okay with employees dating each other, it felt weird to want to date one of my own. It didn't seem like a good example to set. Not to mention how little my parents would be thrilled by it.

Besides, the whole outing had really been more of a business meeting, an area I was good at. So, maybe that was all it was. And yet, I had never wanted a meeting to last all day like today. There was something about Lacy that both intrigued and frustrated me. I loved how she could roll with my cringe-worthy fails at conversation, her snappy comebacks, and her frankness. Yet, she hid so much at the same time, it made me nervous. And she was brilliant. Scarily brilliant. She could have easily pulled off stealing millions from me. I wanted to trust her, but she was still the most likely candidate.

On the other hand, she had had such a sad life. The pain in her eyes made me want to pull her into my arms more often than I had ever been tempted before with any other woman. And it killed me to think I was adding to her pain.

So I didn't know what to do. Which meant I just wanted to hide and work.

Josh pushed his grinning face between me and my laptop. "You have got to see her again!"

I pushed him away. "Did you talk to Gabe?"

Josh positioned himself right behind my laptop so I could see his calculating smile. "That's all taken care of, so that change of topic won't work."

I eyed him. "What did Gabe say?"

"I'll be taking him and Izzy on an excursion tomorrow as my treat."

"So you didn't talk to him."

Josh looked miffed. "They got back almost as late you did and they had romantic plans for dinner and since you forbade me from ruining that, my only option was tomorrow."

He made a good point. "Thanks for respecting their relationship."

"I honestly don't know what she sees in him."

I shot a glare at him. "Leave it alone."

Josh shrugged. "I'm just voicing an opinion. But, I'm more interested in hearing *your* opinion of this girl you met."

"I'm not sharing it."

"How about sharing a romantic dinner with the lady?"

"Go away, Josh."

"What are you afraid of?"

I snapped my laptop shut. "Josh, I did what you asked earlier. Now, do I what I ask and leave me alone. I have a big decision to make and I need peace and quiet to do it."

Josh shot me a penetrating glare, then raised his hands in defeat. "As you wish."

"Thanks," I muttered, re-opening my laptop. Once I heard Josh leave, I pulled up everything the investigators had sent about the crime. If Lacy hadn't done it, then I needed to figure out who did.

Her offer to help popped in my head, but I shooed it away. I was already in hot water with this mess. Letting one of the suspects see all the evidence didn't sound like it would make anything better.

Except... she was really smart. And another pair of eyes could help. It had taken another employee of mine, after all, to spot the theft in the first place. I hadn't been quick enough.

I rubbed my temples. Maybe I wasn't as prepared to take over a major corporation as I had thought. But my father's heart wouldn't have lasted if I hadn't stepped in.

With a sigh, I focused on the information, going over it step by step, but my eyes kept wandering to my phone. I was rarely this spacey. Not even when I had that girlfriend who I knew would please my parents. Still, this process would be a lot more fun with someone.

Um, where did that thought come from? I liked working alone.

But she was so quick on her feet. And her snappy responses were fun.

I wasn't going to get any work done, was I? Fine. I'd call her. But it was for work and to help prove her innocence. Any other reason wasn't allowed to be thought about.

Chapter 13

Lacy

I STOOD OUTSIDE ONE of the fancy restaurants on the upper deck of the boat, peering through the glass like some stalker.

David wasn't there.

I moved to the railing and stared out at the dark sea, berating myself. Why was I even looking for him, roaming the decks like a ghost? The whole island thing had been awkward and work-related.

But it had been fun. I still chuckled at how ridiculously nervous he could get. For someone so rich and powerful, he could be endearingly insecure. And he had been interested in my lame past. For the first time in my life, I had spoken about my parents without someone recoiling in disgust.

Oh, he could be someone I could end up liking a lot. Which would be stupid. The only reason he paid attention to me was because I was a suspect in a crime, remember?

Well, not entirely. He had praised me. Like, hardcore praised. Even had offered a promotion on the spot. I could have had a whole new life in New York City! But those stupid stolen millions had been in the way. And then I had to mess everything up by offering to look at the data.

What had I been thinking? Those crime TV shows were adamant that suspects should never be allowed to see the evidence. I bet I had ruined all the trust that had been building between us because I had asked to help.

But at the same time, I would love to see the evidence. I knew I was the easiest suspect, but once I was out of the picture, the evidence should lead to the real culprit pretty quickly. I mean, if my Dad, who had spent a lifetime perfecting his art, could be caught, then anyone else could, too.

"Well," Josh's voice drifted to me, "if it isn't the gorgeous Lacy."

I gripped the railing, wishing I had kept moving instead of moping like some forlorn puppy for a man who probably hadn't spared me a thought since he had left me. Now I was easy prey for Josh again.

But, maybe David was *with* Josh?

I put on my best smile and faced Josh, then fought to keep my smile alive when I saw Josh was alone. So much for that plan.

"Did you enjoy the island?" Josh asked.

I had a feeling that whatever I said would get back to David. Maybe Josh was here like a spy to figure out what I had thought about everything?

If so, then that would mean David thought about me more than I had hoped. That made me way too giddy.

"I did. David was very nice to show me around."

I expected a flippant response from Josh or maybe for him to chide me for not spending the time with him instead, but I did not expect the utter confusion on his face. "*You* were the one David was with?"

Oh, that did not sound good. This could mean two things: David saw me only as a mere gifted employee he was forced to be with or Josh knew of my past and perhaps thought I was acting like my dad and romancing my victim. "It was for work," I said in a rush. "He had some issues that I helped him with."

Josh's eyes narrowed. "But he showed you around the island?"

Oh, no, now Josh thought I was lying. Why did the truth have to be so complicated? "He saw me walking and offered me a ride."

"To where?"

I really didn't want to explain how I tricked David into going to the lighthouse. I was already in hot water—this was just going to make it worse. Yet, if I didn't tell the whole truth and this got to David, he might take it as proof that I was guilty. "He—"

"Lacy!" Izzy cried.

I might struggle with my so-called friendship with Izzy, but at that moment, I was thrilled to see her. She was the perfect distraction for Josh with that low-cut evening gown hugging her curves just right. Her heels clattered along the deck as she rushed toward me, but her gait stopped once Josh turned around, facing her. Her eyes widened in surprise, then she shot me a look that bordered suspiciously on congratulations, as if I had made a conquest with Josh.

Why was Izzy always so concerned about scoring with men?

"Hi, Josh!" She stepped close to him, far closer than I think a woman dating another man should have done.

"Wow!" Josh relaxed against the railing and let his gaze flow down Izzy's body. "You look stunning."

She giggled. "Thank you!" She swayed back and forth to show off more of her black gown. "Gabe's promised me a romantic dinner and I can't wait."

She should be waiting somewhere that was not next to a gorgeous, rich man like Josh, in my opinion. I might not know Gabe very well, but I didn't think jealousy would look good on him.

Oh, but what would it look like on David?

What was I thinking? David would never be jealous of me. More likely he'd be ashamed.

"You should get the lobster," Josh said. "It's better than the famed ones in Maine."

"Is that so?" Izzy asked, her eyes turning to me as if I would know the answer.

"I've never been to Maine," I said. "Or to this restaurant." I indicated the expensive one behind Izzy.

Josh leaned toward me. "Maybe I could fix that?"

Being stuck in his company would ruin any meal. "No thanks."

"Oh!" Izzy clapped her hands together, showing off several of the rings on her fingers. "Josh, you should invite her along to do zip lining with us. Then it would be like a double date!" She gave me a wink as if she was being helpful. It was like she was purposefully failing to understand I had no interest in Josh.

"I'd rather not." I hoped my tone was firm enough to get through Izzy's thick skull.

"Why not?" Josh asked, my warning clearly not getting through his massive ego. "Your lack of swimming skills can't be a factor here. Are you afraid of heights?"

The temptation to use that excuse burned on my tongue, but it would be a lie. "That is not why I don't want to go."

"Of course she wants to go," Izzy exclaimed. "You need to be ready by eleven. Josh, you should pick her up from her cabin. Lacy gets lost easily."

I mentally groaned. Izzy had once witnessed me getting lost in a mall.

Josh looked amused. "She does, huh? I'd be happy to pick you up, then."

I opened my mouth to shut this whole thing down but Izzy suddenly shrieked, "There's Gabe! Gabe!" She waved as if we were in a crowd, but since there were only a few other people around, Gabe would have to be blind not to spot us.

I turned and decided Gabe was blind—his eyes were only on Izzy, his look of delight obvious. I was surprised, myself. That was a nice suit Gabe wore. My mind automatically began calculating the possible costs. Add the suit along with the fancy restaurant and the shopping earlier today and the number was getting quite big. That senior management position must pay really well.

Gabe wrapped his arms around Izzy and pulled her into a hungry kiss, then whispered something in her ear that made her giggle. I had wondered what jealousy might look like on Gabe or David, but I should be wondering what it would look like on me. Being adored like that? The ache was probably on my face.

I cleared my throat. "Well, it's been fun, but I need to go."

Gabe jerked in my direction, the surprise quickly turning into a dismayed sneer. "Lacy, I didn't know you had made it back in time to catch the ship."

I raised an eyebrow. How did he know about that?

"Josh has invited Lacy to go ziplining with us!" Izzy exclaimed. "Isn't that the best news ever?"

Gabe's smile was stiff. His voice had even less enthusiasm. "The best."

"I never said I was going—"

"Nonsense," Izzy said. "You don't have to play coy with us. We're all friends, right?"

I wished I had never met any of them at this moment. "I need to go. Excuse me." I scurried away before they could stop me and I retreated to my cabin, determined to never step out again for the rest of the night and maybe even all day tomorrow if it meant saving me from being roped into going with that group. I sank into the chair by the small table attached to the wall and stared out the small window. It wasn't as good as up on the deck, but at least I had peace and quiet here.

The slow blinking of a light on my cabin's phone caught my attention. A message? Who could possibly want to leave me a message? David?

Ha, yeah right. More likely it would be Josh to bully me into going tomorrow. If so, I had no desire to listen to it.

I ignored the message and pulled out a book to read instead, but curiosity finally got the better of me and I dialed the numbers needed to retrieve the message.

"Hi, Lacy." David's voice.

I dropped the phone. It just slipped right through my frozen fingers. I scrambled to retrieve it but his message was over by the time I had the phone back to my ear. I frantically redialed to repeat the message.

"Hi, Lacy." David's voice was a lot deeper over the phone. Deliciously deep. "Thanks again for the macros. We didn't get a chance to talk, but I think I'll take up your offer to see if you can help me figure out who the culprit is. Call me if you agree."

I checked the time. He had left the message over two hours ago. I had been roaming the decks looking for him while a message had been waiting for me this whole time.

Three seconds later, the operator put me through to David's suite and I waited impatiently for him to pick up.

"Hello?" That was not David's voice. That was Josh's.

I hung up. My panicked mind couldn't think of anything else to do. I paced my cabin a few times, then picked up the phone and made sure I clearly said David's full name to the operator. But it was Josh who answered once again.

"Hello?"

I should change my voice. Go high? Go low? No, both would be considered a lie. Honesty was the way I swore to live my life.

"Hi, Josh." I hoped the dread wasn't obvious in my voice. "Can I—"

"Lacy! Of course you can change your mind."

David

I snapped my head up as Josh's voice shattered my concentration with the mention of Lacy's name. I had been expecting her call for a while but nothing had prepared me for her to be talking to Josh first.

"I'd be happy," Josh continued, grinning at me as if he'd won a bet, "to pick you up at eleven."

I rose to my feet, the blood pumping through me. I had only two thoughts: When had this happened? And why was she going with Josh and not me?

"Sorry?" Josh's triumphant grin began to droop. "Oh, I see. Yes, he's here." His grin lit back up again as he put a hand over the phone and waggled his eyebrows at me. "And he looks like he's going to kill me."

I ripped the phone from him and Josh laughed, moving out of harm's way. I gave myself a shake. I didn't want my anger to transfer over the line. I didn't even know why I was so mad. Josh was just egging me like usual, so why did it bother me so much this time?

"Lacy?" I asked.

"David? Hi, you left a message—"

"Yes, over two hours ago." Why did I mention that? This was her vacation—she was not obligated to respond to my beck and call.

"Sorry, I, uh, was busy."

Not a frank response. She didn't trust giving me the real answer and that made my blood pump again.

"But," she continued, "I would love to take up your offer if it's still available."

I blew out my breath, trying to calm down. I was acting so weird. "Yeah, it is. Come up to my suite tomorrow around eleven." Josh should be gone by then for his activity with Gabe.

"S-sure." She didn't sound very sure. "Until tomorrow then."

"Yeah, until then." I hung up.

Josh promptly burst out clapping.

I shot him a glare, having a feeling he was up to something and I didn't want to endure it. "Leave me alone, Josh."

"Are you kidding? We have to celebrate! You, David, just invited a single girl to be all alone with you in your grand suite."

I froze. I hadn't even considered how the request would look—it had seemed logical to me—but Josh was right. No wonder Lacy hadn't sounded very sure. That was a very unprofessional thing to ask of an employee of mine!

Me and my stupid mouth. I grabbed the phone. "I need to call her back."

"No, you don't." Josh swiped the phone from me. "This is progress!"

"This is a lawsuit ready to happen."

Josh frowned. "How?"

"She's my *employee*, Josh."

"Who you spent four hours with today."

I groaned. So he had found out. "You arranged for this, didn't you?"

Josh laughed. "I didn't say one word. You made this mess all on your own."

He was right, but that did not make me feel any better. "Give me the phone. I need to fix this."

"She'll be fine. Have the butler provide breakfast and then hover. That will give both of you a witness and stop any lawsuit."

I liked that idea a lot. Except for one thing. "It can't be breakfast. Eleven is too late for that."

"Eleven is perfect for breakfast."

I rolled my eyes. Only Josh would think that. But there was still something else I wanted to know. "Why were you going to meet her at eleven? I thought you had that thing with Gabe."

"I do. I had invited Lacy to come along."

"I didn't tell you to do that."

Josh plopped onto the couch. "You didn't tell me about lots of things today. Luckily, I found someone more willing to talk."

I rubbed my face. "Lacy told you, didn't she?"

"She sure did."

I hesitated for a full second and I saw Josh's grin grow. He knew exactly what I was tempted to ask. I growled at him. "Just spit it out."

"Nope. You have to ask."

I didn't want to give him the satisfaction so I stomped over to my laptop instead. But I couldn't concentrate worth beans. "Fine. What did she say?" I shot over my shoulder.

"That it was for work, that she helped you with something, and that you were very nice."

I did not feel any better. I didn't even know what I wanted. I was her boss, forcing her to work while on vacation, and I was accusing her of being a thief. Her calling me nice was more than I deserved.

"Not what you wanted?" He piped up.

"Shut up, Josh." I did not need him to rub it in.

"So what's your plan of attack tomorrow?"

"She's going to help me figure out who the thief is."

"That does not sound romantic at all."

"She's my employee. There are protocols, and this is not following any of them. And"—I rubbed my face—"She's a lot smarter than she lets on. It's possible if she starts pointing the finger at someone and I can verify for certain it's not that person, then maybe that will give me the solid proof that she's the thief." I didn't want that to happen, but I had to keep my head. Everyone involved was someone I did not want to be guilty. My feelings were only a hindrance to this process.

"So you're setting her up?"

"I'm giving her the benefit of the doubt," I shot back.

"Sounds like she should be going with me. She'd be safer."

I turned to glare at him. "Stay out of this."

Josh just grinned. "If you say so."

Chapter 14

Lacy

THE MAP ON MY phone had to be defective. That had to be the reason why I still couldn't find David's suite.

Defeated, I headed back to the elevators to try again. I must have gotten turned around somehow. Why did this ship have to have rooms that all looked the same? Suites should look different, shouldn't they?

"Lacy!" Izzy called and I fought not to groan out loud.

"Where's Josh?" she peered around me as if he was hiding in my hair.

"I'm not going with you all. I'm going somewhere else."

"Oh!" She glanced at my phone. "That's the number for David's suite!"

How did she know that?

"I see what you're doing," she continued as she pressed for the elevator. "Playing the two rich guys against each other. That's brilliant!"

"I am *not* doing that."

"Of course." She drew her finger across her mouth as if zipping it up. "Your secret is safe with me. And I'll drop some good stuff for Josh." She stepped into the waiting elevator. "He'll be ready to eat out of your hand when he gets back."

"No, don't. I don't want either of them."

But Izzy just winked and smiled as the elevator doors closed, leaving me alone in the hallway. I squeezed my eyes shut, wishing I knew the secret to get Izzy to listen to me for once. It was like she lived in her own world and nothing could penetrate it. My mother had lived like that. Granted, she was usually drunk as well, but it still was very frustrating.

Sometimes, I wondered if my dad's flair for crime developed as a way to get away from his wife.

Not wanting to dwell on those unhappy thoughts, I focused on my useless map, then checked it twice with the map in the hallway before taking off once more. This time, I had success and knocked on David's suite.

The door opened to a man I had never met. He was dressed in the type of outfit I would imagine a butler would wear.

"Miss Armstrong, I presume?" he asked.

"Yes?"

"This way, please."

Oh, he *was* a butler. I had no idea suites could come with one.

I entered the suite, then fought to keep the awe off my face. The place was huge! I could fit my cabin in here at least three times, and that didn't include the door leading to what I presumed was the bedroom. I was glad the door was shut. When David had asked me to meet him here, I hadn't exactly wanted to go. It sounded like a bad situation to end up in. But David didn't come across as the type of guy who would do something like that. Josh, on the other hand... but he wasn't the one I was stuck with, thank heavens.

A sudden thought popped in my head. My dad was like Josh. What if David was testing to see if I was going to try to seduce *him*?

Ha, he was going to be *very* disappointed. The only kiss I had shared was with a boy I used to play with at the bar my mother liked. Even if I hadn't sworn off such actions due to my dad, I was ten years rusty at this. I probably couldn't seduce a pillow at this point.

"Lacy." David rose from where he sat at the table. I realized there was food laid out.

"You didn't have to provide lunch," I said. "There's a buffet with tons of food on this ship already."

"The food is from the buffet."

"Oh." And he had it delivered personally to his room? Well, someone was a bit spoiled.

The butler helped me into the chair and I tried my best to look like I was someone more important than a lowly employee who was only trying to clear her name. I expected the butler to disappear, but he continued to hover, ready to fill any of my glasses at the slightest indication. Weird.

Our conversation was stiff with the butler around, sticking to light topics like the weather and the activities offered on the ship.

"I've gone to a few shows," I said. "They're pretty good. But you've probably seen them all dozens of times."

"No, not really," he said. "I usually just hole up in here and work."

"Really? The whole time?"

He nodded.

And I thought I was a workaholic. "Why do you even bother coming, then?"

"My father always did and it was a tradition I wanted to keep."

"So he worked the whole time, too?"

He shook his head. "He tried, but my mom would drag him out. We were always kicked out during the mornings, though. That was his quiet time to work."

It took me a second to realize he was referring to his siblings. "You all came as a family?" The picture of him with his perfect family floated before my eyes. It must have been so nice to have grown up in a normal, stable family.

"Yeah," he answered, "every year until I hit my teens."

I cocked my head. "What happened then?"

He shrugged. "Life got in the way. Had enough?"

I had finished a while ago, but when I nodded, the butler cleared my plate. He worked on clearing the rest of the table while David pulled out his laptop. He fiddled with it for a second, then slid it over to me.

"This is the information given to me, and these are the accounts that were affected."

I gulped. He really was trusting me with everything. I had better not ruin it.

Reading the overview first, I then started cross-referencing. Out of the corner of my eye, I noticed David kept his eyes on me as if watching for any sign of betrayal. This really was a test. And my hands were shaking. But I was innocent! Stop being so afraid!

But something was wrong. I cross-referenced again, dread forming in my stomach. I checked a third time. Then a fourth.

I had always thought the reason they picked me was because of my history of lies. That I had just been in the wrong place at the wrong time and the real culprit would be easy to find. But that wasn't the case at all.

"I'm being framed."

David leaned toward me. "Explain." That was his commanding voice, the one I'm sure he used when he was not pleased with his lowly subjects.

"These transactions"—I pointed at the spot in the spreadsheet, but my hand shook so hard, I doubted he could understand where I meant—"they all have my authorization code."

"You saying you didn't input them?"

I wished I could claim that. "No, I remember them. The requests showed up in my inbox about every three days. I remember thinking they were strange, but they had the required signatures, so I entered them in."

"Why didn't you voice that they were strange?"

"Because I didn't want the attention." My stupid web of lies. They made me stay quiet. Which meant the thief had a perfect victim to use—and they must have planned for that. They picked me specifically because they knew I'd be too scared to do anything. So I stupidly filed all of the fraudulent claims for months, trying my best to keep my head down, never realizing I was digging my own grave.

However, there was a possible escape.

"I scanned those claims. You should be able to access them. I didn't always check the signatures very well." Probably not the best thing to confess at the moment, but it was better than him believing I stole three million. "So many people signed off on the money requests that I only checked to make sure there was a signature. C-can I have access to those files? Maybe the signature—"

"My team's already checked those. They've confirmed they were forged."

The blood drained from my face. I went to jail for forgery. It was the one area I had excelled in helping my dad with. That hadn't been in the overview document, but I didn't think for a second that David wasn't aware of that fact. He probably hid it from me to see what I would do.

"This has me all over it." The words tumbled out my lips. "If I didn't know it wasn't me, even I would believe it was me." The world seemed to spin, darkness closing in. David was a saint to even consider giving me a benefit of the doubt with all this evidence. But it didn't matter. I couldn't fight this. Not with my history of lies. I was as good as gone.

A strong arm wrapped around my shoulders and righted me. I hadn't even realized I was falling. Had I been about to faint? I wanted to faint—to disappear from this reality and somehow wake up in one where I wasn't heading to jail.

"You don't look good." David's voice was a whole lot closer, but I couldn't figure out where it came from. All I could see was the laptop with all the evidence stacked up against me.

"I-I think I should lie down." The world was tilting again. But I suddenly was propped up against something solid. I relaxed. The solid wall was warm and smelled of lavender. Two arms surrounded me, making me feel safe, just like when my mom would hold me when I had a bad dream.

"Do you remember who dropped off that request?" David's voice sounded awfully loud and weird against my ear and there was an echo coming from higher up.

I scrunched my face, trying to remember. A warm hand was rubbing up and down my back, making it hard to concentrate. Everything was so hazy. I just wanted to snuggle deeper into these warms arms—

Alarms rang. Those arms were David's. I was in *his* arms.

I shot up straight. He let go at once and raised his hands as if saying he meant no harm.

Everything inside me wanted to be wrapped up by him again. But wouldn't that count as trying to seduce him? Wasn't this a test? And I was failing, wasn't I?

I covered my face. "I'm sorry—"

"You looked terrified," he cut in. "I was trying to help."

"O-okay." I didn't know what else to say. All the evidence was against me and now I had just tried to seduce him. Why wasn't he calling the cops already?

"Do you remember who dropped off that request?"

That question sounded familiar. Had he asked that already? Oh, yeah, when he was rubbing my back. Oh, that had felt so good. No, stop it. I had a question to answer! "Uh, no. It was always there when I came into work."

I heard the laptop get dragged over to him. It didn't go very far. He had scooted his chair directly next to mine. Wow, did I miss a lot of details earlier. But my mind was still in a fog. It was like after I had panicked in the water. I was exhausted.

"I'll ask my team to pull up the security footage," he said. "We'll see if we can track down who kept dropping off that request."

Was he... still believing I was innocent? I didn't want to raise my head from my hands. I was too afraid I would cling to him in a hug of desperation. Or burst into tears. Or both.

Chapter 15

David

I STARED AT LACY. She sat hunched over, clutching her face as if she was heading for a guillotine in the next minute. I desperately wanted to pull her back into my arms, to somehow relax her so she would no longer look so shattered, but the way she had reacted earlier—that terrified pull away—made me keep my hands to myself. I was her boss *and* the man accusing her of thievery. My touch was only making things worse.

Focusing on the email instead, I wrote out the request, then sent it. Lacy never once moved during the entire process. I couldn't leave her alone like this.

"Hey, how about we go do something fun?"

There was a long moment of silence. "Fun?" she finally breathed through her tense fingers.

"Yeah. You've never been to this island, right? I'll give you another tour and you can make fun of my lack of touring skills."

She slowly uncurled herself to look at me. The horror still lingered in her eyes, but amusement seemed to be growing. "You sure?"

"Yeah. Hey, Al!" I called. The butler had withdrawn to the wall but he immediately stepped forward at my call. "Arrange for a car in about twenty minutes."

He gave a slight bow. "Of course." Then he was off.

"That is so weird," Lacy whispered, her eyes on the retreating butler. "You have a real butler. Like in the movies."

I chuckled. "You want him?"

"No way. He'd have nothing to do when I'm in jail."

I didn't like her defeated tone. I knew everything pointed to her, but her horrified panic had been as real as her panic in the water. She was innocent. I would swear all my money on it. Which meant someone I trusted wasn't only stealing from me but was using her to their advantage. That made my skin crawl. I really hoped whoever it was either had a really good reason for this or was evil to the core so I could pummel them without impunity.

But first, I needed to cheer up Lacy. I disliked seeing her like this.

"It's not a done deal yet. You have two things in your favor. One, they can't prove the forgeries are yours." They had assumed at first, but when I had asked for them to dig deeper after Lacy had insisted she was innocent, they'd found it didn't match the forgery style she had used when she was younger. That didn't mean she was automatically out of the clear since she could have changed her style, but it did mean she wasn't instantly guilty. "Second, they can't find proof you've spent any of the money."

She straightened a little. "You saying my avoidance of shopping is my sole saving grace?"

Ah, there was the frankness I loved. She was becoming more like herself. "Yep."

"Well, what do you know. Being dirt poor could be a good thing after all."

I laughed and put my arm around her shoulders—then realized what I had done and let go.

"Uh, after you." I indicated the door.

She had tensed at my touch and now marched to the door. I had worked so hard to relax her and then messed it up seconds afterward. What had I been thinking?

I hadn't thought; that was the problem. It had felt so natural to hang my arm around her shoulder, to pull her in like we were girlfriend and boyfriend. But she had nearly suffered a panic attack. She probably thought I was abusing a bad situation, using her to my advantage. The idea churned my stomach. I needed to clamp down on my stupid feelings fast.

We made our way to the dock and I noted she made an effort to keep a large space between us. Yeah, she totally thought I had exploited the situation.

My butler was waiting for us at the dock with bad news. The car would be another five minutes. He relayed the news as if I were going to fly off the handle for being forced to wait five minutes. Great, now Lacy probably thought I had a habit of terrifying butlers. This day was getting worse and worse.

I rubbed my face for a second, then stopped. A sign proclaimed the use of ATVs for rent.

"Hey, Lacy." I pointed to the sign. "What about doing ATVs?" I hadn't been on one in years. It would be nice going on some of the old trails I had done with my sisters.

Lacy did not look thrilled. "I've never driven one."

"Can you drive a car?"

She nodded.

"Then you'll get the hang of it pretty quickly. Come on." I pressed a wad of bills into the butler's hand. "Let the driver know we changed our mind. Or you can take the car and go somewhere."

Al's face lit up. "Really?" That was the first un-butler thing I'd seen him do.

"Yeah." I clapped him on the back. "Have fun."

"Thank you!"

"Anytime." I headed for the ATVs, Lacy following me. They had plenty for us and gave a quick breakdown of the rules and instructions. They handed out helmets, which I put on in seconds while I straddled one ATV, then looked back at Lacy. She stared at the helmet as if it was a foreign object.

"What's wrong?" I asked.

"I'm not sure I should drive." She held up the helmet. "I'm still shaking."

Oh, she was right. She was more in shock than I had assumed. And I had charged on ahead without even realizing it. What was wrong with me? I wasn't normally this distracted. But neither did I normally keep reminiscing about holding a woman. Sheesh, I was losing my mind.

"We can go back for the car," I said.

"You gave it to the butler."

She was right. "I can call for another one."

"You have *two* butlers?"

I grinned. "I will have to do the actual calling this time. I know, it might be a bit much for me."

That got a chuckle out of her. "Be careful. You might sprain a finger."

"That would be the worst." I pulled out my phone and started dialing, but frowned when I went to voicemail. "They must be busy today."

"What if I joined you on your ATV?"

I looked at her in surprise. "You sure?"

"They said we could ride double. You okay being my chauffeur again?"

I grinned. "Yeah, I think I could handle it."

At least I thought I could. But as she climbed on and slid her thighs alongside mine, I realized I had not thought this through. She was way too close to me, her scent of clean fabric wafting around me. My heart rate skyrocketed, pumping like mad in my ears. I waited for her arms to wrap around me next, but she leaned back and gripped the handles on the back.

Not wanting to admit how disappointed I was by that, I started up the machine and merged onto the road. Since I had promised a tour, I dictated random anecdotes that I could remember off the top of my head about the areas we passed until I reached the trail I wanted.

"It's going to get rough," I warned as I turned off the main road. "It might be easier if you hung onto me." It was out before I could stop it. Me and my stupid mouth. I didn't dare turn to see how she was taking it, so I waited with bated breath, not sure what she was going to do.

Chapter 16

Lacy

DAVID COULD *NOT* BE serious. I'd been resisting hanging onto his strong body since I had made the stupid mistake of getting on this ATV with him. I had already acted like some hapless female earlier, forcing him to embrace me and hold me up. Clinging to him now would only make that image worse.

But he was right. The terrain was rough and my arms ached from trying to hang on as I leaned back, away from him, trying to create as much space as possible on this small vehicle. I was trying to maintain some sort of dignity, but you know what? My reputation was already destroyed and this was, no doubt, going to be my last vacation for a very long time. I might as well enjoy it to the fullest.

I took a deep breath, then slid my arms around his upper waist. Wow, the man had muscles. I could feel them tense as he moved with the machine. Since I didn't know what else to do, I plopped my helmet-covered head onto his back. He was talking again, but I no longer cared what he said. Clinging to a guy like this while surrounded by lush tropical forest, seemingly in the middle of nowhere? It was like I had been transported to heaven. So this is what a happy ending could taste like. I never wanted it to end.

But the ending came when we emerged out of the forest and headed up to the top of a large hill, giving a breathtaking view of the island and the surrounding ocean.

"Wow," I breathed against his back. Even though I knew the fantasy was over, I kept my arms around him, my head on his back. He hadn't shaken me off yet, so I was being an idiot and refusing to make the first move. "How'd you find this place?"

"This spot is famous."

"How so?" I'd been enjoying the random stories he had shared of the places we had passed. They usually involved the antics of him with his sisters and I had a feeling this one would be no different.

"Because this," he continued, "is where I tried to impress my sisters with some cool moves and ended up flipping my ATV on top of myself."

That made me pull away to give him a no-nonsense glare. "Please don't do that."

He laughed. I loved it when he did that. "Relax. I'm not thirteen anymore. And I learned my lesson. I broke my leg in three different places." He touched his leg at the three different spots.

"That must have been awful. I've never broken a bone in my life."

He turned to get a better view of me. "Never?"

I shook my head. "And I don't want to change that fact, so don't get any ideas."

He laughed, producing the effect I wanted. "I won't. You can trust me."

Trust. Yeah, I trusted him. More than I should, really. But he had given me a chance at innocence when no one else should have. Not with that mountain of evidence against me. He was a good man. A really good man. And I had no chance with him. That hurt more than the fear that I might soon end up in jail again.

He launched into another story about his sisters and I found myself laughing. It felt so easy, sitting close to him and talking about life as if we had no cares in the world.

"You know," I began, "you never really mention your parents in all these stories. Where were they?"

He frowned for a moment. "Not sure. Doing something boring, I guess? They wanted us gone anyway and I had lots of adventures to find." He grinned at me.

That did not sound like him at all. "I never took you as the daring type."

His grin died. "Really?"

"You're not daring in business. All our transactions and acquisitions are safe bets."

He gazed at me as if I was a puzzle. "First you're a genius at computers, now you're a wiz at business?"

I waved my hands. "I'm no wiz. I'm just an accountant."

"Then why do you think I only make safe bets?"

I frowned for a moment. It had always been a feeling of mine as I processed the orders of my branch. "I think... well, I think because of my... dad." I shot him a look, worried that was the wrong topic to bring up. But his face registered only genuine curiosity.

"Go on," he said.

Talking about my dad made me nervous so I stared out at the ocean. "As you know, I helped him in his, uh, business acquisitions." That was a cop-out way to describe him scamming people, but it sounded so much better. "And I was good at numbers. I remember looking at the, uh, prospects," Victims, really. "And I'd pick the easier ones but my dad, he always liked a challenge. He'd pick the not-so-safe ones. Since I got that promotion, I've been attending the meetings of our branch and, well, we never seem to go after a challenge, and I got the impression from everyone that that decree came from the top."

I held my breath, waiting for his response. I was sure it wasn't going to be good. My parents had never liked it when I pointed out a problem of theirs. But David remained quiet, staring out at the sea.

"I'm sorry. I shouldn't have—"

He held up a hand. "I'm processing."

I had no idea what that meant so I shut my mouth and tried my best to exercise patience.

"I think," David began after what seemed like an eternity of silence, "you're right."

I stared at him, stupefied. "You do?"

He rubbed his face. "My father had his first heart attack when I was fifteen."

I gasped. For some reason, I had assumed that David hadn't suffered hardship. Boy, was I wrong.

"It was a huge shock," David continued. "I was just a normal kid one day, goofing off with my sisters and friends, and then the next day, my father was in the hospital, barely hanging on, and I was staring at the fact that I was the oldest child, the only son, and my family needed me to be a man. I had to be reliable and responsible like yesterday. I think... that's when I stopped being daring. I couldn't afford to fail."

My childhood hadn't been great, but I had never been in charge of anyone else. Yeah, I kind of was the caretaker of my mom, but no one blamed me when she succumbed to her alcoholism. Neither did I have younger siblings to uplift and bolster during that ordeal. I only had to deal with my own pain.

I put a comforting hand on his back. "I'm sorry. That must have been awful." I hesitated for a second, but my curiosity got the better of me. "When did your dad have his second attack?"

"About three years ago."

That number sounded familiar. "That's when you took over the company, isn't it? You did it to save your dad."

He nodded. "But I'm not doing a great job at it, apparently. I got stolen from, you're being framed, and my dad is itching to take over again. It's like he can't realize he's driving himself to an early grave."

"People can be really stubborn," I said, my thoughts on Izzy. "But, to be fair, I don't think you're doing a terrible job."

He glanced at me. "You just said I'm not daring enough."

"I said I didn't see you as daring. I didn't mean to imply that was a bad thing. You have kept the company doing well. It didn't fall apart when you took over."

"True."

"And you gave me a chance despite everything saying I'm the bad person here. Thank you very much for doing that."

He frowned. "Do you have any enemies? Someone who would want to frame you like this?"

I hadn't considered that angle. "I... don't know? I mean, I don't think so, but... I did help my dad. We did hurt a lot of people. But no one has come up and told me they recognized me from that time."

He faced the sea again. "Did you ever realize you were doing bad?"

I froze.

He caught my reaction. "You're probably going to evade that, aren't you?"

Normally, yes. But, he was choosing to believe in me. He deserved the truth.

I let out a long sigh, my eyes on my legs. "When I... look back at it now, I can see all the times where I did sense I was doing wrong. However, at the time, I didn't recognize the warnings." I switched my gaze to the ocean. "I trusted my dad. Adored him, really. He had been the one who made sure I had enough to eat, who brought me cool gifts, who helped me deal with my mom's problems. He was always on the road, a traveling salesperson—or so he would call himself—so I rarely saw him, but I knew when he *was* at home, I would be taken care of.

"When my mom passed, he asked if I would go on the road with him. I jumped at the chance. Being with my dad twenty-four-seven was heaven to me. He gave me all the attention my mom never did and I just... just couldn't grasp the concept that someone so good to me would be doing bad to others."

I glanced at David, wondering how he was taking the confession. No disgust lined his face. Only sadness.

"I can see how that would get confusing," he said.

"It was beyond confusing," I muttered. "Especially since he used the same loving tactics on his victims. I remember one family, a really happy couple with two girls around my age. They had money problems. My dad promised he could get them out of it, even gave them some cash to pay off their immediate bills and such, so they trusted him and handed over all their assets..." I had to swallow, the regret and pain boiling up inside. "I still remember their faces of joy when my dad walked away. They believed he would return with wealth untold, having no idea they'd never see him again. I remember sensing it was wrong, that if the roles had been switched, that if I had been one of those girls in that happy family... I still remember their names. Elizabeth and Lacy."

He raised an eyebrow. "Is that why you picked Lacy as your new name?"

I nodded. "They were fun to be with. I liked them. Especially Lacy. She was so happy. But my dad and I, we walked away, purposefully *ruining* them." I covered my face. "Their happy faces... they haunt me to this day. I hate that I... I had helped to destroy them."

David wrapped an arm around my shoulders and pulled me against his chest. A part of me insisted this was not at all appropriate between a boss and an employee, but I didn't care. I wanted comfort and he was offering it. I pressed my face against his shirt and let him rock me in silence, his hand stroking my back. If only this could never end.

But my suspicious brain started to wake up. This really was not appropriate. And hadn't he done this earlier, when I was freaking out? Was I somehow succeeding in seducing him without even trying? Maybe I was more like my dad than I thought. Which meant I would end up hurting this amazing man.

I pushed away from him. "I think we should head back."

Chapter 17

David

IT TOOK ALL OF my inner strength not to fight Lacy when she pulled out of my arms. It had been so comfortable, holding her like that. She had such a strong, yet fragile strength and she had been put through the wringer at a young age. Yet she seemed determined to put it all behind her and be a better person. It amazed me. I wanted to be by her side and make sure she made it.

But she pushed me away.

I couldn't blame her. She had a lot of pain and I was the cause of some of it. I needed to find out who had framed her. I just wished it wasn't someone I trusted and liked. But if she could survive being betrayed by her dad, then I could endure this.

I did as she wished and took her back, though I hoped she didn't notice that I took the long way. She had immediately wrapped her arms around my torso once we started going and I stupidly ate up every excuse to keep her hugging me like that.

But all good things had to end and I was forced to return the ATV.

"What are your plans for dinner?" I asked as we headed up the ramp. I knew I should let her be, but I didn't want her out of my sight. It was like I had turned into a forlorn puppy, desperate for any attention she sent my way.

"The buffet." She cocked her head at me. "Do you ever go or do you always have your butler bring the food to you?"

Was that an invitation? "I usually do the butler route, but I could make an exception."

Her eyes widened. "Oh, I-I wasn't trying to invite you."

So much for that invitation. “I wasn’t assuming as much.” That was a lie but she looked so uncomfortable, I didn’t want to push the issue. “What are your plans for tomorrow?” Did that have a desperate tone in it? I hoped not.

“I don’t know.”

“I could give you another tour.” Yeah, that definitely had a desperate tone to it. What was happening to me?

“I think I’d rather go on my own tomorrow.”

That hurt. A lot. I must have really messed things up today. I shouldn’t be surprised. There were so many problems with this relationship. I didn’t even know why I was trying so hard for it.

No, I did know why. I liked her—she had sucked me in the second I saw her in that line. But, like usual, I couldn’t get the woman I liked to like me back.

“Well,” I began as we boarded the ship, “Let me know if you ever think of someone who might be trying to frame you.”

She nodded. “Okay.” She took a few steps, then turned. “Thanks, by the way. I don’t think I said that.”

That sounded like a goodbye. I didn’t like that at all, but I had nothing to say, so I forced a smile. “Anytime.”

She smiled back then walked away, leaving me alone in the hallway, watching her until she turned the corner. I rubbed my face in frustration. I needed a plan. And standing like a dejected idiot was not a good plan. If I figured out who was framing her, she would have to talk to me then. And Josh should be back from ziplining with Gabe.

Except I hoped it wasn’t Gabe. He was a good employee and I knew how hard he worked to provide for his three kids. If Gabe was the culprit, it would hurt more than just him, not to mention destroying the budding romance with Izzy.

There was one good thing. When Lacy mentioned the request showed up before she arrived at work—and with the signature being forged—it meant it could be anyone now. It didn’t have to be someone I trusted.

Now to see if my team had dissected the security tape yet.

Lacy

That was the hardest walk I had ever done, but it had to happen. There was a hunger in David's eyes, the same type of hunger Gabe exhibited toward Izzy. And while everything inside me craved that hunger, that only confirmed my worst fear.

I had somehow turned into my dad.

He had made countless women look at him the way David now looked at me. I wasn't even sure how I had done it. I was a nobody and yet I had captured the attention of my wealthy, gorgeous boss who should never have given me a second look. Which meant I had power.

And that scared me.

My father hadn't always swindled. The court case against him declared he preyed on his first victim when I was five. And it had been a small scam, nothing big. But it had been an opportunity that had landed in his lap. And instead of doing what was right with the trust given him, he abused it.

What if I did the same?

I didn't want to, but I hadn't wanted David to look at me like my dad's victims, either. So, for David's safety, I needed to put as much distance as possible between us. That way, I wouldn't be tempted to... to... well, *use* him. He could give me everything I had ever wanted: charges dropped, a fresh start in New York City, a prestigious job, and the perfect boyfriend by my side.

But I didn't want it through fraud. Except I didn't know how to make this relationship legit. None of his attention to me made sense. So the only answer had to be that I was bad and he needed to stay away from me.

Since I didn't know if David would randomly show up for the dinner buffet, I waited until near closing before I slipped in. A quick scan confirmed he wasn't there. With a sigh of relief, I grabbed a plate and began filling it.

"Lacy!" Izzy was by my side in seconds. "I'm so glad I caught you! I knocked on your cabin but you weren't there."

"I was out."

"I know." Her grin was conspiratorial. "And I want to hear all the juicy details!"

I wanted to snap and insist there had been none, but since that would be a lie, I abandoned filling my plate and retreated to a table instead. She followed me, however.

"So?" she prodded, propping her elbows on the table and dropping her chin into her clasped hands.

"How was ziplining?" I asked.

She squealed. "So much fun!" She regaled me with more details of ziplining than I ever wanted. "You should have come," she added. "I bet Josh would have been more interesting then. He got boring and only wanted to talk about Gabe's work. Who wants to talk about work while on vacation?"

I hoped that meant Josh didn't fall for whatever grand plan Izzy had had in mind.

"What of David?" Izzy pressed.

"I helped him with work." That was technically true for the beginning part.

Izzy's excitement died. "That's it?"

"It was the sole reason he wanted to see me." Also completely true.

"But how did you turn it to your advantage?"

By apparently going into a panic. David had changed a lot after that. But I wasn't going to mention any of that. "I'm not you, Izzy. I have no interest in abusing my relationship with David."

She laughed as if I had told a joke instead of the truth. "You say the strangest things! I bet that's why David can't keep his eyes off you. You're strange and guys like him love abnormalities."

Was that how I was doing so well with David? How ironic that my desire to be completely honest was backfiring. Maybe I should act more like Izzy?

The thought made me gag. She was too sickeningly dense. I'd rather avoid David than have to act like her.

"You know," Izzy continued, "that reminds me. Gabe said the strangest thing about you today, and Josh didn't look happy when he said it."

That piqued my interest. "What do you mean?"

"I told Gabe he was full of it, but he kept insisting it was true. He claimed you weren't as you seem and that the apple didn't fall very far from the tree. Weird, right?"

I dropped my fork. Was *Gabe* the one framing me? I knew he disliked me, but I had assumed it was because he didn't think I was good enough to be his friend. But... what if I had said something when we were once buddies? Something that led him to investigate my real past.

But why would he steal money from David? Gabe didn't seem the type to do that. Or was he a better actor than I thought? I hoped not. He had kids—children who trusted him. Why would he do something so stupid that would destroy his kids in the process?

I rose to my feet. "I need to go."

"Now?" Izzy asked, rising as well. "But we haven't properly chatted. It's like you're always avoiding me."

I didn't want to confirm that was the utter truth. "We don't have a lot in common."

"That's 'cause you never let me get to know you! We should do a spa day tomorrow. Unless you're with David again?"

I was so glad I had no plans with David. "I'm on my own tomorrow."

"Perfect!" She linked her arm through mine. "Spa day it is!"

"No, Izzy." I removed her arm. "I want to be alone."

She scoffed. "No one wants to be alone."

"You have Gabe. Spend the day with him."

"But he doesn't like the spa. Oh, I know! How about we go shopping?"

I definitely wasn't doing any shopping. Not since that was my one saving grace for not being accused of stealing all that money.

I paused. Gabe had been spending a lot of money recently, hadn't he? I had assumed his senior position paid enough for that, but what if he had another source of income?

"Have a good night, Izzy." I hurried away, relieved that she didn't follow. Once I was in my cabin, I paced the small space for several minutes, trying to avoid the cabin's phone.

Honesty demanded I should tell David my suspicion about Gabe. But it didn't seem fair to point the finger at Gabe when I had no proof other than his new spending habits. And wouldn't David had already checked Gabe? Gabe was one of my supervisors, after all, and would have been one of the forged signatures.

There was another problem with calling David. It would mitigate the distance I wanted to maintain between us.

I had a better idea. Picking up the phone, I asked for Gabe's cabin. It dialed twice before he answered.

"Hello?"

"Hi, Gabe, it's Lacy."

"What do you want?" That was definitely a growl.

"I'd like to talk—"

"Not now. I'm busy."

"Tomorrow, then?"

"Is this important?"

"Gabe, you don't like me. Do you think I'd call you for fun?"

There was a pause. "I'm taking Izzy for a spa day at that resort the cruise is offering. I'll be stuck there all day. If you find me, we can talk." He hung up.

Well, it wasn't a grand plan, but at least I had something.

Chapter 18

David

FRESHLY SHOWERED, I WALKED out of the bedroom and found Josh sound asleep on the couch. I had given up waiting for him last night and, judging by the fact he was still dressed from the day before, I guessed he'd turned in only hours ago. I had a lot of questions to ask, but I had learned during our teen years that Josh was a monster if woken up too early.

Sitting down at my makeshift desk instead, I started working. Lacy had mentioned I wasn't daring in business, so I had decided to look over the past year's missed opportunities and evaluate which ones I should have dared to seize. Making a new spreadsheet for the job made me wish Lacy was with me. She'd probably design a faster way to do this entire process. Maybe she'd agree to see me today if I promoted her? Or would that count as bribing?

I rubbed my temples. Lacy had been on my mind nonstop since she left my side and for the life of me, I couldn't seem to get her out of my head. And each new scheme I came up with to see her today seemed to sound more and more desperate. I needed to respect that she wanted space.

It was three hours before Josh finally stirred.

"Late night?" I asked.

Josh grumbled something unintelligible and rolled over. It took another hour before he finally sat up.

"Your typing is very loud," he growled.

"I find it very soothing," I quipped.

He muttered something that suspiciously sounded very unkind toward me while he plodded toward the guest bathroom. Another hour later, Josh came out, whistling and acting more like his chirpy self.

"I hope," I began, "this good mood has nothing to do with Izzy."

He stopped his whistling long enough to glare at me. "I'll have you know there are more women on this ship than Izzy. Besides"—he plopped onto the couch; the butler had tidied it up for sitting while Josh was in the bathroom—"I have changed my mind about Izzy. I'd rather spend today with Lacy."

I clanged my keyboard, my heart rate skyrocketing. "You talked to her?"

"Don't hit me," Josh warned. "I was joking. But"—he shot me a grin—"now I know how well your day went."

I was sure my glare could have murdered him. "Did you talk to her?" The idea that Lacy might be two-timing had blossomed at Josh's words. I believed she was innocent, but she did once excel at swindling people. Maybe she was duping me.

Josh's amused smile faltered. "Did you two have a fight?"

"You didn't answer my question."

Josh's grin re-ignited. "You know, I don't think I've seen you this jealous of a girl before. And before you kill me, the answer is no. I didn't see her at all yesterday. I was with Izzy and Gabe as ordered by you, and then I found more interesting people to recharge with."

"I'm not jealous." It came out exactly like a sullen kid would say it. I glowered at my laptop, mad that Josh was right. I barely knew Lacy and yet, she somehow had managed to consume all my thoughts. I'd dated girls before but never felt so possessive as this. And she wasn't even mine. Yet. I hoped.

No, I shouldn't hope that. She was my employee *and* being framed. I needed to fix things first. Though I didn't know how to fix being her boss. She was too talented to give up nor did I think she'd appreciate being fired so I could date her.

But I could at least fix the framing part. However, my team had gone through the tape. Everyone who had passed through the hallway leading to Lacy's cubicle had a legit reason to do so. Which meant I was back at square one. I had my investigators start speaking with everyone who had passed through that hallway but they had noted Gabe was one and they were struggling to reach him.

"What did you discover about Gabe?" I asked. I really hoped Gabe wasn't involved in this—he had been one of my most reliable employees—but if it wasn't him, then I was out of people to consider.

"He's a good man," Josh said and I didn't know whether to sigh in relief or frustration.

"His kids sound amazing," Josh continued, "and well-rounded despite their mother dying so young."

"Cancer, right?"

"Yeah. As for Izzy, I don't know what Gabe sees in her. No, actually, I know exactly what he sees. He's a middle-aged man being charmed by a gorgeous young lady. But her heart is not in the relationship."

I didn't like the sound of that. Gabe had asked my advice on whether to date Izzy since she was a subordinate of his and I had told him to pursue it if Izzy was fine with it and if they followed the protocols. And every time I had seen them, they had seemed ridiculously happy together.

"Are you sure?" I asked.

Josh rolled his eyes. "Let's just say, if I had made a pass, she'd be in my lap right now. But since I promised you I wouldn't break them up, I'll let him figure it out."

I didn't like that at all. Izzy had seemed so in love. Was I that bad at reading people?

"What else did you learn?"

"A whole lot about Lacy."

My heart rate skyrocketed again. I mentally cursed the girl's ability to affect me so easily, especially since I could tell by the way Josh was smiling that he had noticed my instant reaction.

"Stop dragging it out," I spat out. "Just tell me already."

He shook his head. "This is way too much fun! You should see your face whenever I mention Lacy."

"Josh," I growled.

He laughed. "All right. They both seemed eager to talk about her, but neither had a good opinion of her."

That didn't sound good. Maybe I didn't want to hear this.

No, I needed the facts. It might help balance my skewed feelings. "Go on."

"The consensus is she's very quiet and private. Closed off and rude, is how Gabe called it while Izzy claimed Lacy was just very shy. Izzy's been trying to get Lacy out of her shell for over a year now and is determined to succeed."

Considering Lacy's past, I could see why she fought to keep to herself. "Anything else?"

"Gabe insisted Lacy was not to be trusted."

I raised an eyebrow. "Why's that?"

"He wouldn't go into the specifics. I think you'll have to get those. He's taking Izzy for a spa day today but I think he's going to be bored to death. You can probably catch him wandering the resort. Unless you have big plans with Lacy?"

"I'm not seeing her today."

Josh eyed him. "So you two *did* have a fight."

"We did not."

"Let me guess. You still think she's the thief and she didn't like the idea of dating someone who doesn't trust her."

"That wasn't the case at all."

"Then what happened?"

"Nothing." I focused on my laptop. "She wants space and I'm giving it to her."

Josh moved to the chair next to me. "You're giving up."

I avoided his gaze. "I'm doing no such thing."

"Yes, you are. You're immediately assuming you're at fault when a relationship is no longer going the way you wanted and backing off so you don't get hurt."

I silently fumed for a second. Lacy had accused me of not being daring enough in business and now Josh was basically claiming I did the same in relationships. Was I really this afraid of failing?

Yes. Yes, I was.

I reached for an excuse. "I really don't think it's a good idea to chase after someone who does not want to be chased." I didn't read people as well as Josh. I'd hate to be the guy every girl dreads interacting with 'cause he's clueless they're not into him.

Josh rolled his eyes. "David, girls *always* want to be chased. Even Izzy, who was practically begging to be in my lap, would still want to be chased. So get out of here and go get your girl."

I glowered at my laptop. What was I supposed to do? Show up at Lacy's door? I needed an excuse and I didn't have one.

Josh eyed me for a moment. "Fine. If you're not giving chase, I will."

He was goading me but it worked. I was on my feet and out the door before I realized it. Except I still didn't have a plan.

Gabe. I would talk to him first and then figure out what to do about Lacy.

Lacy

Why was it so hard to find a famed resort?

I blew out my breath in frustration as I stared at the picture of a map I'd taken with my phone. I was lost again and I knew it. If only I had a cool enough phone plan so I could access the internet and have it dictate the route. That was how I survived back home.

With a sigh, I retraced my steps, heading back to the dock. I had tried asking a few locals for help, but since I didn't speak their language, their help only seemed to get me more confused. I should probably just wait for Gabe on the ship. This island was much bigger than Grand Turk—I could end up seriously lost and miss the ship's departure time if I continued trying to find that resort.

The sea roared to my right as it came into view and I ventured onto the beach, but not too close to the expansive water. Just seeing the water reminded me of my panic. The people around me, however, milled about, lying in the sun or playing in the waves. Even little kids played, unafraid of the constantly moving water.

It was unfair. Here I was, stuck and alone, while everyone could play without fear. It seemed like a metaphor for my life. There were so many things I wanted to do, but fear kept holding me back. I had fought so hard to be free of my past, but it still plagued my every move.

"Lacy!" Josh cried.

I jerked in surprise as he waved at me. A group of ladies surrounded him, but his eyes were on me. Hoping he was just acknowledging my presence and nothing more, I gave a short wave, then resumed walking toward the dock.

Josh, however, excused himself from his fans and aimed for me. "Where you headed?"

I wasn't exactly thrilled to be accosted by Josh again, but hey, perhaps I could put him to use. "Here." I showed him the picture on my phone.

He frowned. "You're on the wrong side of the dock for this."

I groaned. I knew I had gone the wrong way. "Can you give me very easy instructions on how to get there? I get lost easily," I added when he raised his eyebrows in surprise.

"It's a long walk. It would be better if you took a cab."

I shook my head. "I'd prefer to walk."

"I don't," he said as he steered me toward the street. "I'll get us a cab."

"You don't have to take me—"

"I have a feeling you'll never get there if I didn't."

He was probably right. "I'll pay for the cab, then."

Josh laughed. "Nope, you won't."

I bristled at that. "You don't think I can?"

"I think you don't like me so every favor I offer, you want to shoot down."

I sputtered for a second, taken aback, but when he grinned at me as if he knew he'd scored a point, it spurred a comeback. "I refuse to owe you anything."

"I never said you did." He waved a cab and opened the door for me. "But you can still dislike me since I'm not doing this to be nice. I'm doing this 'cause I'm selfish."

I eyed him. "What do you mean?"

"Get in and I'll explain."

He was manipulating me—just like my father used to do. Principle demanded I deny giving him an inch, but at the same time, curiosity demanded the answer. Plus, I did need help getting to that resort.

Shooting him a glare, I got in the cab. He followed me, then spouted something in Spanish to the driver.

"You speak Spanish." I stated.

Josh shrugged. "Only enough to impress the ladies. David speaks it better. His younger sister is fluent."

Judging by the smug expression on Josh's face, I had a feeling he'd brought up David on purpose. Adding in that he had mentioned he was being selfish by taking me to the resort, I suddenly had dread wash over me. "David is at the resort, isn't he?"

Josh's smugness melted into confusion. "You were not aware of this?"

I shook my head. "I'm going to see Gabe."

"I was not aware you were friends."

"We're not. I'm going..." I hesitated. Josh seemed to be good friends with David, but I didn't know how much he knew about me being framed. It didn't seem right to spill those details. But I didn't want to lie. That would definitely get back to David and I needed every ounce of honesty to ensure David still believed me. "I guess I'm going to see why he dislikes me so much."

"An odd reason to randomly hunt him down during a vacation."

This was another reason I disliked Josh. He saw through me too easily. "I can't give the real reason, okay?"

"You could have come up with a better reason than that, though."

"I don't like to lie."

"Interesting. Gabe believes otherwise."

I cringed. I knew Gabe disliked me, but I didn't know he thought so poorly of me. Then again, I had divulged a fake past when our friendship was blossoming—him now knowing the truth probably destroyed any good opinion he might have had of me. "I... have not always been honest. But I'm trying to change that."

Josh grinned. "Well, then, for starters, you can tell me why you seem to dislike me so much."

I rolled my eyes. "That's easy. You're arrogant and pushy." And too much like my dad, but I kept that to myself.

Josh shrugged. "Some women like it. What about David? Is he too arrogant?"

I wasn't taking that bait. "I'll keep my opinion of my boss to myself."

"Ah, so I'm arrogant *and* untrustworthy."

"You know that's not what I meant."

"It is exactly what you meant. You don't think I have the best intentions."

"I think you like playing people and I'm currently your most interesting game," I shot back. "But I want the game to stop."

The smug look was back. "You're very smart. I can see why David likes you so much."

Where did that come from? "Tell him he can't."

"Let me guess. Because you're poor, live in different states, or believe his family will be appalled by you?"

I hadn't even considered any of those. "Thank you for giving me *more* reasons as to why he needs to stay away from me."

Josh's smug look died but the cab pulled up to the resort, so I darted out of the car before he could say another word. Hurrying inside, I headed for the check-in desk and inquired if they knew Gabe and Izzy's whereabouts. The clerks could only give me a general area to head for, but one was kind enough to lead me to it instead of making me figure it out on my own. The resort was huge, with towering stacks filled with rooms while pools of all sizes lay scattered around as though the ocean, less than fifty feet away, wasn't enough.

The clerk deposited me at the check-in area for the spa and I began my inquires once again, only to stop as two men stepped into the area. Gabe was the reason I was here, but I barely noticed him with David next to him. David wore nothing special—shorts and a t-shirt—but just the sight of him made me giddy. Which was stupid. There was no possible happy ending between us. Even if I wasn't being framed and had scamming genes, Josh had listed a bunch of reasons as to why this would never work, and if Josh thought David's family would be aghast because I was poor and an employee, I couldn't imagine how they would take to my criminal background.

Gabe's serious expression changed the second he spotted me, replaced with muted anger. That wasn't a good sign. Then again, David was probably asking him questions regarding the stolen three million. No doubt Gabe thought I was the one who had directed David toward him.

I waited with dread for David to find me, torn with hoping he would light up when he saw me but also knowing he shouldn't. But Gabe said something and the two men headed back into the hallway before David ever saw me.

I was crushed. Then mad I was crushed. I had wanted to avoid David, hadn't I? So Gabe had done me a favor. Though I wasn't going to let him know that.

Chapter 19

David

"Are you sure she sabotaged you?" I asked.

Gabe nodded. "She recently did these macros—"

"I know of them."

"Well, once I saw those, I knew she had to have purposefully ruined that project of ours."

I didn't understand the project he spoke about—it seemed to be something their old boss, Sam, had assigned the group to speed up the processing of a routine task. This was before my time as the CEO, when I had been helping my father with acquisitions instead of running the business. But I could tell that whatever Lacy had done still bothered Gabe a lot. Which would give him the perfect motivation to frame Lacy, but his earlier denial had seemed as genuine as hers.

"I figured," Gabe continued, "that there's no way she could have messed up that badly unless she wanted to make sure I would never get promoted."

"But why would she target you?" That was the core point I had yet to understand.

"I'm a family man. I have kids."

"Yes, you said that before. But I don't understand why that means Lacy would specifically seek to harm you."

"Sir, do you not know of her past? She went after families."

I had read the reports, but none of them had come to that specific conclusion. "I thought her father—"

"Not just her father, sir. Lacy would make friends with the kids, then introduce her father to the parents. Then clean them of all their assets.

My oldest is near her age. I'm sure she was hoping to do the same thing to me."

"But her father is in jail right now."

"She's got a roommate who's versed in crime, too."

This was news to me. "Who is it?"

"Sarah Williams. She works for you, too."

How many past criminals did I have working for me? "With Lacy?"

"No, different department. She works with Izzy. But Sarah is the reason Lacy got the job. She highly recommended Lacy with her fake resume. Never batted an eye over the lie. I was there. I saw it all. And I've been keeping an eye on Sarah, too, sir. I would bet my kids' college fund that Sarah was Lacy's accomplice in the stolen millions. They've both been looking for an easy victim. I'm sorry it was you, sir."

I blew out my breath. My gut told me Gabe wasn't lying. I'd known him for years—he wasn't acting differently than before. But his words put Lacy in a really bad light. And I didn't like that assessment.

Facts. I needed facts. My emotions couldn't be trusted right. I needed to push away everything and focus solely on the facts.

"Thanks, Gabe. I appreciate what you told me."

"I'm happy to be of help. You're the best boss I ever had."

I smiled. "Thanks. But I'm taking away your time with Izzy."

"Not really. I'll be joining her for a massage in," he checked his watch, "five more minutes."

The memory of Josh's observation of Izzy came to mind. "How's that going, can I ask?"

The grin on his face was probably as goofy as mine when Lacy was in the room. "Really good, sir."

"Glad to hear it. Have fun." I walked away, hoping that Josh was wrong about Izzy. The problem was that Josh was rarely wrong about women. He had a knack of seeing right through them. But Josh also believed Lacy was innocent. And if Josh was wrong about Izzy, he might be wrong about Lacy.

I came to a fork in the path, the left leading to the front of the resort, the right to the main pool. I turned right; it was longer and I needed time to think. Once at the pool, I sat down on one of the many benches surrounding the pool and, since I had forgotten my laptop in my suite—Josh's fault—I pulled out my phone and typed a request for my investigating team to look into one Sarah Williams.

If anything that Gabe said proved to be wrong, then at least I'd know not to trust anything he had said. But if it proved true, then I might have a very tough decision in regards to Lacy.

I sighed, rubbing my face. I really didn't want her to be guilty. What if all of this was due to the roommate? Maybe she was the one framing Lacy? I liked that idea. Then I didn't have to get rid of Gabe or Lacy.

There was one more good thing to come out of this. I had a legitimate work reason to see Lacy again. Which meant she couldn't refuse to see me.

The thought made me grin and I sighed. I really had it bad for her, didn't I?

Lacy

Since Gabe knew I wished to speak with him and he had clearly seen me, I had moved to a chair that gave me a clear view of the hallway but, thanks to the various plants strategically placed about the area, prevented him from seeing me easily.

David emerged first and headed toward the main part of the resort. It wasn't until he was out of sight that Gabe strode out of the hallway, heading directly for me. I rose at once, my speech ready to go. I wanted this over as fast as possible.

But Gabe spoke first. "You're fired."

My carefully arranged speech went up in smoke. "You can't—"

"Yes, I know. You have David wrapped around your finger so tight that you'll get the job back in ten seconds. But don't you think for one second that I don't know you're trying to frame me for stealing millions we both know you stole, to ruin me like you've done to countless families before me, so hear this: I will do everything in my power to bring you to justice, no matter the cost." With that, he whirled around and stomped back to the hallway.

"Wait!" I tried to follow but a resort employee barred me from entry. I didn't have a wristband like Gabe did. If I wanted to follow, I'd have to pay.

Furious, I marched out of the spa center and took whatever path I found, not caring where I went. How dare Gabe get to say his piece and not let me say anything? How dare he fire me without even giving me a chance to explain! I needed this job! My resume was full of lies—if I tried to get a job with my real skills, no one would take me. It was the whole reason I had lied in the first place, and look where it got me. I did not want to end up in this mess again.

And Gabe was right. If I told David about this, I'd have the job reinstated—David would give me a chance, unlike Gabe. But if that happened, working under Gabe would be a nightmare. He'd probably tell everyone about my past and get them to drive me out. Maybe even include Sarah in this mess and get her fired, too. Or maybe he'd frame me for something even worse than stealing three million. Assuming he had framed me in the first place.

Why did I keep ending up in terrible situations? Why couldn't life give me a good deal for once?

Actually, it did give me something good. David. If I worked it right, I could have that promotion instead.

But no, that would require charming him and I wasn't going to do that. No matter how miserable I ended up in the end.

The path I had taken ended at a large pool with several slides and dozens of kids running around, yelling and laughing. I stopped in frustration. I had no job, I was still being framed, and now I was lost in a fancy resort. All I needed was to miss the ship to make this day the worst of my life.

"Lacy?" It was David's voice.

Nevermind. This day was now ten times worse.

"What's wrong?" he asked.

I didn't dare face him. My emotions were a mess and getting wrapped up in his arms was far too tempting. I wanted David to fix everything, but his fixing would only make things worse.

"I'm lost." It was the only thing I could think of to say that was also true.

I heard him stand up. He must have been sitting on one of the many benches facing the pool, probably working on his laptop. I had no idea why he would consider a big pool filled with rowdy kids running around was conducive for work, but I wasn't going to ask any questions. It would encourage a conversation and I just needed to get as far away from David as possible.

"Lost?" His voice indicated he was standing directly behind me. The temptation to lean back into him hit me so hard, I wrapped my arms around my torso and took a step forward. A bad move since it moved me closer to the pool's edge. The panic started to rise, but if I moved backward, I'd be in David's arms.

"I'm trying to find the exit," I said. "I get lost very easily. I even got lost trying to find your suite on the boat the other day." I was rambling. My brain was overloading. I had death before me and safety behind me, but going backward wouldn't fix anything. Nor did it help that kids were running around, yelling and laughing. Couldn't everyone just be quiet and leave me alone for one minute?

"Hey—" he touched my shoulder.

I jerked forward. Stupid move. I had no more forward to go. Now I was going to add drowning to this horrible day.

But a hand caught my arm, stopping my fall. David had saved the day. However, neither of us expected the teenage kid, his attention on catching some ball, barreling into us.

I was in freefall for two seconds, then the hungry waters surrounded me, engulfing me. I screamed but only bubbles came out. I flapped my arms. I kicked. But no matter what I did, I only went down, not up. I could see the sun shining through the water and the plentiful air above, but I couldn't reach it. I was drowning.

Strong arms wrapped around my torso and my legs and suddenly I was in the air. I gasped for it, frantically refilling my lungs. It felt so good to breathe. I never wanted to be in water again.

"You okay?" David asked, his voice dangerously close to my ear.

It took me a second to realize why. He was carrying me in his arms, above the water. With a jolt, I realized the water was only waist-deep for him. If I had just put my feet down, I could have stood up on my own.

"Put me down." We were fully clothed, now drenched to the bone. I was sure I looked like a fool, being held in David's arms. All I needed was for Gabe or Izzy to walk by and they'd think I did all of this on purpose.

David set me on the pool's edge. I gripped the stone for all its worth.

"Are you okay?" he asked.

"I'm sorry. I should have stood. I wasn't thinking. I'm sorry—"

His hands abruptly cupped my face and tilted it up until I was staring into those loveable brown eyes. "You're in shock. Breathe."

I would rather be kissing him.

Whoa, that thought woke me up and I shook myself free of his hands.

"I'm okay." That was a lie. My whole body shook as if I was suffering a personal earthquake.

He heaved himself out of the pool, the water running like mad down his legs, and sat next to me. "You don't look okay."

"You're all wet." Wow, was I Captain Obvious or what? But my brain wasn't functioning again. I really should never touch water again. It had a horrible effect on me.

"You're wet, too," David countered with a small smile. "But I think we'll survive."

"Everyone's looking at us." I sincerely hoped Gabe or Izzy were not here yet.

"Not so much anymore. It's an exotic resort; I'm sure they've seen crazier stuff. But since we're here and already wet, how about I teach you how to swim?"

He must be joking. But when I stared at his face, I couldn't find a hint of joviality. "Please don't tell me you're serious."

"You nearly drowned in waist-deep water—"

"I know," I groaned and ducked my head.

He chuckled. "It's because you panicked. Your fear made you unable to think straight. I've seen it many times. But if I could give you some basics, you shouldn't freak out if this happens again."

I shook my head. "I never want to do this again." I pulled my legs out of the pool to prove my point.

"You can't avoid water for the rest of your life."

"I did it for twenty-five years," I shot back.

He smiled at that. "Okay, yes, but I don't think that's a healthy way to live."

"It's a perfectly normal way to live. Besides, we don't have swimming suits."

"It will be fine. And if there is a problem, I know the guy who owns this resort. But I want to teach you some basics. For instance, don't scream underwater."

I eyed him. "You heard that?"

"Sound does travel in water. But screaming releases the air in your lungs and you need that to float."

I had no idea what he was talking about.

"Watch," he said as he eased himself back into the pool.

He took an exaggerated breath, then curled himself into a ball and went under the water. A second later, his back bobbed on the surface. Then he uncurled himself. "See?"

I didn't see anything other than he had performed magic.

"Try it." He beckoned me to enter the pool again.

A good chunk of me wanted to refuse. But a larger part wanted to pull off that magic stunt, too. He had made it look so easy—just like everyone else around us did. What if it really was that simple?

I tried to pry my fingers loose from the stone, but they wouldn't budge. Though my mind understood the water wouldn't go over my head, a part of me screamed I'd perish if I touched the water again.

"Here." David was in front of me, his hands out. "Just lean toward me. I'll catch you."

No, no, he was cheating. This wasn't fair. I had a ridiculous reaction of feeling utterly safe around him. I was supposed to be creating distance, not falling into his arms again.

"I-I can do it." That was supposed to come out in strong, certain tones, but it sounded pathetic. I squeezed my eyes shut and tried to imagine the huge pool was just a giant bathtub. I was going to be okay. I did not have to cling to David for safety. I could be a normal, functioning adult while surrounded by water.

With a shaky breath, I managed to ease myself back into the treacherous waters and planted my feet on the bottom of the pool, but I didn't feel solid. The water sloshed around my waist, pushing at me as if its greatest desire was to make me descend below its surface. Why was I in here again?

Oh, yeah, David. He was stationed directly in front of me, his hands on my elbows, steadying me. Despite all my firm admonitions, my hands found David's wet shirt and clung. To make it worse, I plopped my forehead against his chest. So much for being a strong, independent adult. But being with David made me feel better and that was all I wanted at the moment.

"Good job," I heard David say. "You got back in without panicking."

"That's because you're here," I muttered. "You let go, I'm gonna start screaming."

"It's okay," he said and I could hear the smile in his voice. "My sister was the same."

Oh, yeah. I had forgotten he had helped his sister overcome her fear of the water. "You sure she can swim by herself?"

"Definitely. But it took a while. It's the fear that is the hardest to overcome."

I could agree with that.

"Listen," he continued. "Balloons rise, right? Your lungs act like balloons when you're underwater. Take a deep breath and hold it underwater and you'll rise to the top. Try it."

I didn't know which was harder: willingly going underwater or leaving the safety of David's arms. But I could do this. No, I had to do this. David was right—I had nearly drowned in waist-deep water solely because of fear.

Taking a deep breath, I collapsed into the water. Panic assailed me as fast as the water engulfed me and I frantically stood up. David's hands clasped around my elbows in seconds and the panic died.

"I'm sorry—"

"It's okay," he said. "It will take time. Just try it again."

How was this man so patient? No wonder his sister was able to overcome her fear.

It took two more times before I could stay underwater long enough to wrap my arms around my legs so I wouldn't shoot to my feet again. Holding my breath, I fully expected to sink to the marble pool floor where I'd have to be rescued once again. However, to my surprise, I rose up, my body bopping on the surface.

I uncurled with glee. "I swam!"

David laughed. "You floated."

"I didn't sink. That has to count as swimming."

"It wasn't drowning, I'll say that."

"So, is that all I have to do? Hold my breath and I won't sink?"

"Yeah. The air in your lungs makes you rise every time."

I frowned. "But I can't hold my breath forever."

"That's when you flip on your back and float. Here, I'll show you." He moved closer, putting his arm around my shoulders. "Just lean back—"

"Lacy? David?"

If David wasn't still holding my shoulders, I would have sunk into the water in shame. Not only did Izzy stand at the pool's edge, her head cocked, pure confusion on her face, but so did Gabe, rage on his face. They were both in swimming attire, obviously on their way to enjoy the pool.

No way was I going to be able to explain this away.

"She fell in," David shot out. At least someone was thinking on their feet. He immediately lifted me onto the pool's edge as if I weighed nothing more than the ball those kids were throwing around.

"On purpose?" Gabe snarled.

I wanted to shoot him a glare, but I busied standing up while David hefted himself out of the pool. Water streamed down both of us, our clothes clinging to us in awkward ways. Well, not for David. I didn't think it was possible for him to not look gorgeous. Me, on the other hand? I was pretty sure I looked as pretty as a drowned rat.

"You poor thing!" Izzy threw her towel around me. "Your hair is all a mess!"

"Thanks, Izzy," I muttered. Just exactly what I wanted to hear.

Chapter 20

David

"I'll take care of Lacy," Izzy offered. "You don't have to worry about a thing, David."

"No," I cut in. "Go on ahead and enjoy the resort. I'll get Lacy back to the ship."

Gabe shot me a look of exasperation but I just nodded curtly at him, then steered Lacy away, her shoulders hunched as she pulled the towel tighter around her.

I knew this looked really bad. Me, the CEO, caught drenched with an insubordinate who Gabe knew was being investigated for stealing millions of dollars from me. The look on his face told me he firmly believed Lacy had connived me into the embarrassing situation. But I knew who was truly at fault: me. I was the one who failed to respect her space, too concerned as to why she was so upset and why she refused to tell me about it, and then I was the one who had insisted we remain in the pool so she could learn some swimming basics. Lacy was not going to suffer because I failed to think through the situation yet again.

We reached a stack of extra towels and I handed one to Lacy. She took it without complaint and toweled her hair while I worked on drying my water-logged clothes.

"Oh, no," Lacy said. I glanced over and found her staring at her wet phone. "It's ruined."

I took it from her. Mine was waterproof but hers obviously didn't have that feature. "It could still work. Let it dry completely before trying to turn it on."

"Okay." She retrieved her phone and put it her pocket. "You don't have to get me back to the boat, by the way."

"You claimed you get lost easily." It was the first lie she had told me. Or at least, the first one I could tell was a lie. There was no way she could have been that upset simply because she got lost. And it had shaken me. A lot. I was about to demand an explanation when we got pushed into the pool by that random kid. Then seeing her drown robbed me of my anger. She might spout a lot of lies, but her fear of the water was not one of them.

I could still remember her look of terror under the water, her fruitless attempts to swim, completely unaware that she could stand up and be safe. I hadn't wanted her to look like that ever again.

"If you point me in the right direction," Lacy said, the towel over her hair. "I could figure it out."

I wasn't letting her out of my sight. I had a lot of questions to ask, and her near-drowning still haunted me. Add the fact that I had probably just complicated her relationship with her co-workers and I owed her the courtesy of making sure she got to the ship safely, whether she lied about getting lost or not.

"We'll walk together. With this heat, we'll be dry by the time we reach the ship."

"C-can I keep the towel?" She still had it around her hair.

"Sure." I had no idea why she wanted it but I could always mail it back. Or, since I knew who owned the resort, I could tell him to dock me for it. But right now, I wanted to be moving.

"Lead the way," I said, wondering just how lost she really was.

"Me?" She glanced around the area as if she was trying to find a neon-light lit path. "I don't remember how I got here." She then shot me a look of exasperation. "You think I lied about being lost, don't you?"

So much for that test. "No one gets that upset about getting lost. This way." I strode toward the right and she followed. I waited for her to give an explanation, but she walked in silence, the towel still covering her head. I suddenly wondered if she was using the towel to hide, but I knew how fast gossip moved. While Gabe would keep his mouth shut out of respect for me, I had a feeling Izzy would be gabbing to everyone she knew about the development. There was no point in hiding anything now.

"I did get lost," Lacy said, breaking the tense silence between us. "And it added to my anger, but you're right. It was not the initial reason."

I eyed her.

She shot me a glare. "You can ask Josh. He's the one that helped me find the resort. I had been heading in the wrong direction. Again."

I resisted the urge to pull out my phone and call Josh on the spot, mainly 'cause I knew Josh would give me grief for being with Lacy again. In fact, I wondered if he had hovered near the dock for the express purpose of telling Lacy where I was.

However, that did bring up the fascinating point that Lacy had been trying to find me.

"What did you want to see me for?" I asked.

"What?" She stopped. "I wasn't going there for you at all. I didn't even know you were there until Josh told me."

"Were you going for a spa day?" I knew the cruise had offered it as an excursion, but I also knew the price tag. If she was as poor as she claimed, she should not have been able to afford it.

She shook her head and started walking again. "I went to see someone."

I matched her pace with ease. "Who?"

She pulled the towel closer around her face. "I really don't want to talk about it."

Well, at least she was telling me the truth. But I didn't like her avoiding the question, either. I had no idea who she could have spoken with. She didn't seem to have any friends on this trip other than possibly Izzy. I frowned, trying to imagine those two having a fight. Izzy had seemed gleeful when she'd offered to take care of her, not mad.

I blew out my breath in frustration, wishing I knew a way to force her to tell me what was going on. I could command her as her boss, but that seemed immature on my part.

"Tell me about your roommate," I asked instead. At least I could get answers to that.

But she balked. "W-why do you want to know about Sarah?"

That reaction was how I'd imagine a guilty person to act. Fear was in her eyes and she took a step away from me as if nervous I might suddenly haul her off to jail. My heart sank. Why was she acting like this? I wanted her to be innocent!

"Gabe claims you sabotaged him."

Anger took over her fear. "He's blaming me and you're believing him."

"No, I want answers. He says about four years ago, you two were supposed to come up with a way to increase productivity on a certain project, but you blew your side of the job, robbing him of a promotion."

Confusion crashed on her face for a moment. Then horror dawned. "Oh, the macros..."

At least she came to the same conclusion as Gabe. But that didn't make her look very good. "I take it you *did* sabotage him?"

She pulled the towel over her face and ducked her head. "Not on purpose. I mean, not him specifically."

"I need more specifics than that."

She was quiet for a moment. Was she frantically trying to figure out the best lie to get her out of this?

"He picked me as his partner because we were somewhat friends," she began and I had to lean in to catch her quiet words. "And I had proved to be a hard worker. But... I wasn't ready for all the attention. You know of my web of lies—I was terrified they were about to be exposed. So, I made sure I didn't win. Which, in retrospect, cost Gabe a win, too."

That... made a lot of sense. It fit with everything else Lacy had dropped about herself and it followed what Gabe had told me. That meant both were telling the truth—which meant I was back at square one without a clear-cut villain.

"Do you think," she began, dropping the towel from her face, "that would give him enough motivation to try to frame me?"

She, apparently, thought Gabe was the villain. "He seemed as genuine in his insistence of innocence as you." I paused for a moment. "Is there something you know about Gabe that you don't think I know?" It was only fair to hear her accusations if I had been willing to listen to Gabe's.

"I don't know. I know he hasn't liked me for a long time, but if he believes I sabotaged him on purpose, then now I know where the dislike comes from."

"So you don't have anything on him?"

She was silent for a second. "You told me my saving grace was my lack of spending a lot of money. Well, Gabe seems to be spending quite a bit on this trip."

I hadn't considered that angle. "He does have a lot of savings." I had helped him invest some of it.

"Honestly, I hope it's not him," she said. "He has kids. To be a child and find out your father was not a good man..." She let the sentence trail, but her look of frustration and anger finished it.

I wanted to pull her in, to somehow ease the pain shining in her eyes. Her life had been unfair for a long time.

But she pulled the towel closer to her face as if trying to hide.

"Why are you wearing that?" I couldn't help asking.

"The towel?"

"Yes."

She shrank from me. "I don't want to answer."

Oh, no, she wasn't getting away being evasive over a towel. "Why not? It's not harming anyone and I'm the one that gave you permission to take it off the property, so you can't fear I'll accuse you of stealing it."

She shrank further. "It's really nothing important."

"So then tell me already."

She sighed. "It's my hair."

"What? Does it turn some weird color when wet?"

"No, it frizzes and I wore it down so I have nothing to tie it up with. It's a complete mess."

I burst out laughing. She looked aghast but I couldn't help it. Wearing the towel seemed so much worse than frizzy hair.

"You can't look that bad." I reached for the towel but she moved out of reach.

"Yes, I do," she pouted. It was the cutest thing I had ever seen. Now all I could think about was kissing those pouting lips.

Except she started walking away. She might be wanting space, but I was not in the mood for space. In one step, I caught up to her and yanked the towel off her head.

Whoa, she was right. Her hair *was* a mess. A cute, frizzy, adorable mess I just wanted to entangle my hands in.

She turned around, her eyes wide in horror, and clamped her hands over her hair.

I laughed. "You look fine." I tugged one of her hands away from her hair, then attempted to smooth it down myself. It was a lot silkier than I had anticipated. My hand dug in, loving the feel of it. But that brought her face closer to me. A lot closer.

My heart galloped and my breath caught. We were but inches away. Her wide eyes stared directly into mine like we were caught in a time trap and neither of us wanted out. Then her gaze dropped to my lips. I knew what that meant. And I was perfectly fine giving what she wanted.

I leaned in, the smell of her surrounding me, my hand tipping her head up toward mine. I had been wanting this for sooo long.

But hands pushed against my chest.

"S-stop."

Chapter 21

Lacy

I WAS MELTING—MELTING RIGHT into him. But the vision of Gabe and Izzy when they had seen us in that pool seared my mind, waking me up.

"S-stop." I tried pushing away but he was rock solid, one hand cradling my head, the other around my waist, holding me firmly in place.

"Why?" His voice was low and husky. My resolve weakened fast. He could talk like that all day, please.

"Is it because," that deliciously low voice of his continued, "I'm your boss?"

Ha, I wished that was the only reason. And technically, he wasn't that anymore, not with Gabe firing me. But someone was framing me, deliberately trying to harm me. And I had such a horrible past and no future. No one would understand why he had any interest in me. *I* didn't even understand why he had this much interest in me. But if I gave in, he'd consume me. I would never survive this. But his family and friends would look at me like Gabe and Izzy had done and insist I had conned him. And they'd be right *and* they'd free him from me. And I would have to let them because it would be the right thing to do. But it would leave me more shattered than when the sting operation had closed the curtain on my dad.

"Please let me go."

He didn't move. "You didn't answer my question."

There was too much to be said. My resolve wouldn't last long enough. My knees were already weakening. "I don't want to be played with."

That made him pull back. "You think I'm playing you?"

With several extra inches now between us, I gasped for air. I hadn't even realized I had been without it.

"You have to be." I pushed against him and this time, he let me go. "I'm a nobody in your world. And I've been acting like a helpless female for most of this trip. I'm easy prey."

Oh, what was coming out of my mouth? I was making it sound like he was the villain instead of me. And he looked like I was stabbing him with each sentence.

"I would never do that. Ever."

"But you have no skin in this game." Words were just hurtling out now. I wanted him to hate me. No, I *needed* him to hate me. That way, he'd stay away. And be safe from me. "You have all the power in this relationship. You can control everything about me and I can't do anything about it."

"That's not true. You have a lot of power over me."

I shook my head. I didn't want to hear this.

But he kept going. "Like the fact that I normally focus only on work, but this time, the only work I'm getting done is what excuse I can use to see you again."

He shouldn't talk. It made me want to melt into him again. But I couldn't. This would only end in disaster.

He stepped toward me. "You're all I think about, what I dream about." His hands were in my hair again, his eyes consuming me. "What I crave..." He leaned in. He was going to kiss me if I didn't do something. Anything.

"Money," I murmured.

That stopped him. "What?"

I didn't know where that thought had come from but I ran with it. "Give me money." That was probably the worst thing I could have said. Now I really did sound like a swindler.

But it did the job I wanted. He snapped away from me. "What?"

I didn't want this vehicle, but it was all I had to drive into him. "If you're serious about me, then you'd pay me." Wow, that made no sense whatsoever. I was digging my own grave fast. No way was he going to believe I wasn't the thief after this. But why bother? Gabe had fired me and threatened to make the job unbearable if I tried to fight to get it back. The only other option was to use David and I refused to do that. So I would have to go to jail. I'd been there before. Maybe I'd even get locked up with my dad. Then I could unload all my anger on somebody worthy of it.

David stared at me. "You can't be serious."

"It's called putting skin in the game." I didn't even know where I was getting these ideas. "I need money to pay for a lawyer for when you tire of me and slap me with the swindling charge. So, I demand you pay me for every kiss."

I held my breath, waiting for him to outright refuse or perhaps bust out laughing at my ridiculous charge. But he just leveled his cold, brown eyes at me. "How much?"

Oh, I hadn't thought that far. I needed something so insanely high, he'd never pay it. "A hundred grand. Per kiss."

"That's it?"

Ouch. Apparently what I thought was stupid high was not high enough. How rich *was* this guy?

"Yes." I should have gone for a million. Obviously, this was proof I was not great at swindling. I could have been a millionaire after this relationship if I had been a tad more greedy—assuming he actually agreed to this absurd proposal.

He stared at me for the longest minute of my life. Then he swiped the towel from the sand. I hadn't realized it had fallen to the ground.

"I'm taking this back," he announced, then turned and walked away.

David

I leaned against the window of my suite, glaring out at the endless blue waters. I had taken a cab from the resort back to the ship and had passed Lacy, still walking. Despite everything she had said, a part of me still wanted to stop the cab and give her a ride. And she claimed she had no control over me. Ha.

"Sir?" the butler called out from behind me.

I didn't bother turning around. "Yeah?"

"I was able to confirm that Lacy Armstrong did make it on the ship before it left."

Yes, I had asked him to make that inquiry. I was a total sap for her. The walk from that resort was a long one and she had claimed she got lost easily. Though she should have been able to spot the huge cruise ship by the time my cab had passed her.

"Thanks, Al."

"Would you like me to set up for dinner now?"

"Yeah, go ahead. Did Josh say he would be eating with me?"

"He did not. Should I set a place for him?"

"Sure."

I kept my eyes on the ocean while Al worked on the dinner table, but my ears could only hear one thing: a hundred grand. Lacy had demanded that without flinching. It was a ludicrous amount—a nonsensical demand.

And I had actually considered it.

I rubbed my temples in frustration. I must be going insane. It was the only explanation why I would willingly think of paying a woman a hundred grand just to kiss her. I still couldn't believe she had demanded it. The Lacy I knew would never have done that. She must have been faking who she was the entire time. Then when she knew she had me in her trap, her real self came out.

"Dinner is ready, sir," Al announced.

"Thanks. You can go now."

He bowed. "Yes, sir."

I sat down at the table, a variety of food spread out before me, but none of it looked appetizing. I should have just gone to bed. I was in no mood for anything tonight.

Since I didn't want Al's efforts to be wasted, I dutifully ate a few things, then gave up and resumed my station leaning against the window, glaring out at the sea, my mind going over that last exchange with Lacy. It just seemed the complete opposite of her. Why had she done it? Did she really only care for my money? Had I been duped this whole time?

The door burst opened and Josh bounded in. He stopped when he spotted me.

"Oh! I didn't realize you'd be in here. Don't mind me. I just going to change into something a bit more... inspiring."

That would be an overly priced suit. Josh insisted the ladies loved a man in a tailored suit. Considering he was wearing his favorite Hawaiian shirt and short shorts, it would definitely be an upgrade. I let him do his thing. My mind was too preoccupied to care what Josh was up to.

"David?" Josh called about ten minutes later, no doubt now wearing his fancy suit.

"Yeah?"

"You seem... upset."

That was an understatement. "I'm fine. Go and enjoy your evening."

"Want to come with?"

"No." Making small talk with strangers had never been a forte of mine. Tonight would be even worse because I was sure every face would look like Lacy's. And I had no idea what I would do if I met the real Lacy. It was a toss-up between strangling her for manipulating me so well or paying her for that kiss I still craved.

"What's wrong?"

"Nothing. Go have fun."

Josh's footsteps headed for me and soon he had propped himself against the window, his eyes on me.

"I haven't seen you this shaken since your dad had that second heart attack. What happened?"

"My family is fine. Everyone's fine."

He folded his arms. "What about Lacy?"

I glowered out the window. "She said you helped her find the resort. Is that true?"

"Yeah, she had her map turned around."

"Do you think she did that on purpose to catch your eye?"

He eyed me. "What did she do that's gotten you into disbelieving her again?"

"She demanded one hundred grand if I kissed her."

Josh's eyebrows shot up. "A hundred grand? That's it?"

"Yeah. She should have gone for a million." That was one comfort. Lacy wasn't exceptionally greedy. Unless she knew I'd expect a million and went lower to stun me.

"Did you agree?"

"I'm not an idiot, Josh." I pushed away from the window. "She's been playing me this whole time, absconding with three million, luring me in so I wouldn't prosecute her, then demanding more money just to kiss her."

"So... you didn't kiss her?"

I dropped into the chair by the table. "I said I wasn't an idiot."

"But... you still want to."

"No, I'm done with her. She's a liar and a thief."

"And yet, you can't get her off your mind."

I glared at him. "Do you have a point with all this?"

He sat on the chair next to me. "Did she have a reason for the money?"

"She claimed I had no skin in the game. That I was using her, so she wanted something in return."

Josh whistled. "She does not mince words."

"She's a liar."

"I disagree."

I rubbed my temples. Josh was giving me hope. I didn't want hope. I wanted to hate her.

"In answer to your earlier question," Josh continued, "No, I don't think she was trying to 'catch my eye,' as you put it. I nearly had to drag her into the cab to get her to the resort."

I eyed him. "What do you mean?"

"Let's just say she sees through me unnervingly well."

"Which means she's like you and is skilled at manipulating." Good. I could go back to hating her.

"Perhaps," Josh said. "But I think I messed up and gave her more reasons to avoid you."

I wasn't sure I wanted to hear the rest of this, but Josh didn't give me a choice since he kept going.

"She had no idea you were at the resort and was adamant I didn't try to set you two up. When I pushed as to why, I listed a few reasons that I thought were holding her back. Turns out, I just added to her list."

I frowned. "What were the reasons you gave? Me being her boss?"

"That's too easy to get around, so I went for harder ones like the long distance, her being poor, and, the big one, of how your family would react to her existence."

I groaned. My father might actually have a third heart attack if he knew I was interested in a girl with a criminal history. And if Josh had told her that, no wonder she was pushing me away so hard.

"So," Josh continued, "I think this is my fault."

I shook my head. "She asked for money, Josh. Money! She knows she's under suspicion of stealing millions from me. Why would she pick that? If she really did think the relationship was no good, she would have just said so. She's blunt enough to do that."

"Yeah, but would you have listened?"

I glowered in silence.

Josh grinned. "You know, I bet she used money because she knew it would be the only thing that would get you away from her tempting lips."

The idea that he could be right made me mutter hotly to myself. After all, she hadn't thrown out the money demand until the *second* time I tried to kiss her.

I rubbed my face in frustration. Josh *was* right. "Now what am I to do?"

"The obvious thing, duh. Go find her and insist you can work out your issues. Then kiss her to your heart's delight."

"What if she holds her ground on the hundred grand?"

He shrugged. "Pay it."

"What?"

"David, I've blown a lot more than a hundred grand on a girl. In fact, I've blown more than a couple of *million* on a girl."

I couldn't believe it. "How?"

He raised his fingers and started ticking them off. "Jewelry, high-end restaurants, exclusive clubs, flights to romantic getaways, et cetera, et cetera. If all Lacy is asking is a measly hundred grand, take it. She'll be the cheapest girl you'll ever date."

"It was *per* kiss."

Josh raised his eyebrows. "Smart girl."

"Exactly."

"I'd still pay it," Josh said. "I see it as a fair trade. Girls want money and I want girls. But then, I usually move on quickly. You, on the other hand... the love bug seems to bite you deeper."

"I also don't have access to a trust fund where I can spend what I want. My father would freak if he saw me spending that much on a girl."

"So? My dad's been trying to cut me off for ages."

"I *like* my parents, Josh. I want them to be proud of me."

"That's your curse then. But as for me"—he stood up and clapped me on the shoulder—"I have ladies to impress. Have fun with yours!"

Chapter 22

Lacy

My stomach growled. With the resort disaster, I had missed lunch and now stood in line for the dinner buffet, wishing it was open already so I could then retreat to my cabin. This vacation was such a disaster. I got fired, met the most perfect man, then stabbed him in the heart, which probably ensured me going to jail for a crime I didn't commit. And my phone was ruined. Not that it mattered since my phone plan wasn't cool enough to let me call Sarah without costing me an arm and a leg. I desperately needed to talk to someone about all of this, though. Like maybe even a lawyer. Assuming one would be willing to work for pennies.

I checked over my shoulder again. While I doubted I'd spy David—I had never seen him once at the buffet—I dreaded running into Gabe and Izzy. Gabe would hopefully ignore me but I had a hunch Izzy would want to pump every detail of that embarrassing situation in the pool.

When the buffet opened at last, I filled my plate and scarfed the food down, barely tasting any of it. It didn't really matter. Nothing looked good except the tubs of ice cream and mounds of chocolate. I gathered some of the latter and headed out, preparing for a miserable pity party alone.

"Lacy!"

Nope, not alone. With a muttered groan, I faced Izzy as she hurried down the hallway. She wasn't with Gabe, which meant I would have a hard time shaking her off.

"I'm so glad I found you! Oh, chocolates!" She nabbed one from my pile and popped it into her mouth. "Mmm, chocolate makes any day better."

"Did you not enjoy your spa day?" I asked, more to keep her busy and away from my chocolates.

"It started out great. I wished you had come. Just look at my nails!" She flashed her newly manicured nails, painted a bright red. "And they did my hair." She shook her blond locks, letting them bounce around her shoulders. "They would have done wonders for your frizz, I'm sure."

I resisted patting down my wavy, uncontrollable hair. I had whipped it into a messy ponytail the second I had returned to my cabin, but I knew it was still a mess. Yet David hadn't seemed to mind. The memory of his hands in my hair still plagued me. As well as that near kiss. *Two* near kisses. Why didn't I reject him *after* those kisses?

Because I wouldn't have rejected him at all. That's why.

Izzy was still talking, so I tossed those lovely memories and focused on her words as she gushed about the massage. "But," she continued, "everything kind of fell apart when we came to the pool." She squeezed my arm. "Lacy, I'm so sorry!"

I had been dreading this topic. "I'm fine. Like David said, I had fallen in."

She blinked. "Oh, I wasn't talking about that. But," she leaned closer with excitement in her eyes, "since you brought it up, do give details!"

"I just did. I fell in and David helped me out."

"But you were both soaking wet!"

Telling her that we both fell in didn't sound good at all. But neither did I want to lie. "I panicked and was literally drowning in waist-deep water. He had to drag me off the pool's floor."

"How romantic!" Izzy fanned herself. "To be saved like that. You are so lucky you can't swim."

I eyed her. "I thought you couldn't?"

She waved a hand at me. "I'm not great, but I don't drown that easily. Still, to get him soaking wet like that." She fanned herself again. "That was pure genius!"

"I didn't do it on purpose."

She winked at me. "Don't worry, your secret is safe with me."

"I'm serious, Izzy. That was not planned at all."

"Mmm-hmm." She swiped another chocolate from me. "You're so good with guys. Maybe you can help me with Gabe."

"Gabe worships the ground you walk on. I don't think you need any help."

"Yeah, but he's mad at me right now."

"Why?"

"Because after you two left, he told me that he had fired you and I told him that was the dumbest thing to do. So he broke up with me *and* fired me."

I was flabbergasted. "Izzy, that's awful."

"I know." She sighed as if she carried all the world's sorrows, but then abruptly grinned. "Ooo, now we can spend the whole day together tomorrow!"

I stared at her. Izzy was so hard to follow sometimes.

"We should go shopping!" she continued.

That spurred me. "No. No shopping."

She formed a pout. "But shopping makes everything better."

"I've been telling you this for over a year, Izzy: I don't enjoy shopping. It's stressful."

"You must be doing it wrong, but I can fix that." She plucked another chocolate. At this rate, I wasn't going to have any for my pity party.

"There will be no shopping being done by me. So, if you'll excuse me—"

"Wait!" She grabbed my arm. "You can't abandon me. I have no one else to hang out with. You have to come with me. We'll do whatever you want. Just promise you'll go with me."

I hesitated. "I like seeing new places."

"Perfect! There are these gorgeous waterfalls I saw on some flyers for tomorrow. You don't even have to hike. The trails are super easy. We should go to those!"

I wasn't exactly thrilled to be near bodies of water again. "I don't want to get wet."

"Don't worry. We'll enjoy the waterfalls from a safe distance. So, will you go? Please say you will!"

The plan did sound like something I could enjoy. And she did lose her job and relationship for standing up for me. I kind of owed her something. "All right. I'll go."

She squealed. "You're the best! I'll meet you at your cabin at ten sharp!" She grabbed more chocolates and trotted off, leaving me with just one miserable chocolate for myself. So much for my pity party.

David

Morning dawned bright and early and I glared at it. I had tossed and turned all night long and still had no plan for what to do with Lacy. Nor did it help that the few times I fell asleep, she had plagued my dreams. I had never been so obsessed over a girl before. It was maddening.

I showered and dressed, then tiptoed past the couch where Josh slept. He had come in late again and I didn't want to wake him. Once in the hallway, I made my way to the deck, passing only one other person. At this early hour, I knew I'd have most of the ship to myself.

While I didn't plan on it, I ended up at the exact spot I had first spoken with Lacy. My excuse? It was relatively deserted and quiet. Never mind that I kept hoping she might magically pop up. Though I would have no idea what to say, so hopefully she wouldn't show up.

There goes my indecision again. Muttering to myself, I leaned against the railing, staring out at the sea as if it could give me the answers I needed. Breathing in, I tried to push the emotion away and focus only on the facts.

Fact number one: I liked Lacy. She was smart, quick-witted, and strong. She had depths I wanted to explore. But she also had a history of lying and that scared me.

Fact number two: Someone had stolen three million from me. Despite digging deeper, all the evidence still pointed to Lacy. My gut insisted it wasn't her. However, my gut was biased by fact number one. I needed more evidence to either exonerate or convict her but my team hadn't sent me an update yet.

Fact number three: I had not planned to fall for Lacy so hard. Josh had pushed me to pursue her, but I hadn't thought through what such a relationship would entail, like how my family would react. It bothered me that I had nearly kissed her without any consideration of the consequences. Same thing when I insisted on teaching her how to swim. It was like my sense of caution took a hike whenever Lacy was within my vicinity.

I don't want to be played.

Her exact words. I had scoffed at them, but she was right. I had all the power, blindly pursuing her with no solid offer of a future. Basically, I was treating this like a fling and Lacy had made it clear she had no interest in that.

So, the real question was, should this be more than a fling?

I pulled out my phone and checked the time, then dialed my little sister's number. Jane was an early riser like me, no doubt working on another art piece as the sun rose.

"Let me guess," Jane began, "you killed Josh?"

I chuckled. "It's been tempting, but no. He's still breathing."

"I'm still mad you took him instead of me.

"You had that art show."

"My *art* is required to be there, not me."

"Oh, sorry."

"It's okay. I'll forgive you. Maybe. But tell Josh he owes me."

"'Cause I took him?"

"No, he bet he could keep you busy enough that you wouldn't end up calling me out of pure boredom."

"He did that, huh?"

"Yep, and here you are, calling me. I figured Josh must be either dead or he had failed spectacularly. I wish I had seen the latter."

"I feel I must object," I protested. "I don't only call you when I'm bored."

"You do when you don't take me on that cruise."

"Well, this time, I'm calling for a different reason." I paused, suddenly unsure how to bring it up.

"Are you insisting I guess? 'Cause I have no idea."

"No, it's just complicated. I, uh, met someone."

A crash sounded on her end of the line.

"Jane? Are you okay?"

"You just made me ruin this painting! But that's okay, I'll frame it for your wedding."

"I said I had met someone, Jane, not that I'm getting married to her."

"Uh-huh, and when was the last time you called me up to say you had met someone? Never. So, this has to be big."

"It's... complicated."

"Did you already mess it up? You were never great in the romantic department."

I was starting to regret calling her. "I'm not asking for help to get her. What I want to know is how you'll react if I *do* get her."

"And how am I supposed to answer that if I've never met her?" Jane demanded.

"She's an employee."

"Oh, Mom would not approve."

"Exactly, but that's not the worst of it."

"To Mom, there's nothing worse than you marrying a nobody."

"Yeah, well, this nobody has a criminal past."

Jane sucked in her breath. "Okay, that is worse."

"I know. She's had a terrible life, but it's amazing how she's pushed past it. She has this emotional strength that is inspiring, yet she's so fragile at the same time. I can't decide whether I want to keep her safe or watch her fly. And she's smart. Smart enough that she scares Josh."

"She sees through him, huh?"

"Exactly. I'm sure once she finds her footing, she's going to soar like nothing else. And I want to see it." Badly. Saying it out loud made me realize just how much I wanted to see Lacy succeed. She deserved a chance.

"You really like her, don't you?"

I sighed. "It's insane. I barely know her."

"Yeah, but remember Dad? He knew he was going to marry Mom the moment he saw her. This could be your moment."

"I don't think our parents would agree."

"Don't worry what they think."

"Dad could have another heart attack."

"He's going to have a heart attack no matter *who* you decide to bring home. No one is good enough for their kids. Trust me, I know."

I frowned. "Who did you bring home?" I didn't even know she had liked someone enough to do that.

"It never happened. I listened to Mom and never pursued it. Worst thing I ever did. Don't be like me and do that, okay? It's not worth it. If you like someone, go for it; then tell everyone else to just deal with it."

The pain in her voice reminded me of Lacy. They both had big regrets. If I lost Lacy, would I sound like that?

Yes, I would.

"Thanks, Jane. I needed that."

"Anytime. And remember, I already have my gift for you when you marry."

"I still have to get the girl."

"Oh, good point. Guess I'll throw it away, then."

"Thanks for your vote of confidence," I muttered.

She laughed and the conversation moved to how her art show went.

"But enough about me," Jane announced. "Go get this girl. I really want to meet her and I can only do that if you succeed. So go!"

"All right. Thanks." I hung up, then stared at the ocean.

Fact number four: I had to prove to Lacy I was serious. Agreeing to her hundred grand should do that.

But there was a fact number five: It was too early in the morning to knock on her cabin or even to call her. Maybe if she were an early bird like me it would be okay, but I had no idea if that were true or if she were a night owl like Josh.

I groaned. The next couple of hours were going to be unbearable.

Chapter 23

Lacy

THE PHONE RANG. I ignored it. Izzy had already called me twice this morning, seized with this idea that I was going to cancel on her. If she couldn't believe my assurances the first two times, I wasn't going to bother with a third time. She could show up at my cabin and find out.

I resumed staring at the tiny mirror on the back of my cabin door. Izzy, with her perfect blonde hair and petite figure, made me feel like a dowdy ugly duckling. If I was going to be with her all day, I needed a self-esteem booster. So I wore the flirty, scarlet dress. And it looked amazing on me. I twirled in delight. I might not succeed at outshining Izzy, but at least I wouldn't have to feel beaten. Now if only my hair would cooperate. With all the humidity, my hair couldn't decide whether to curl or frizz. Maybe if I had gone to that spa, they could have taught me how to manage my hair. But then, they probably would have cited products outside of my price range anyway.

I threw my hair up into a messy ponytail, then added some earrings. I was going way overboard, but it made me feel better. I really shouldn't feel such a need to compete with Izzy, though. I mean, after all, David had insisted he had only eyes for me.

Oh, why was I thinking of David again? That was over—move on already!

I touched up my makeup, then checked the time. Izzy was due in ten minutes. Except the phone rang again. I rolled my eyes and marched to the phone.

"Just come over already," I snapped over the line.

"Excuse me?" That was David's voice.

I nearly dropped the phone. "S-sorry. I thought you were Izzy. She's supposed to be coming over. We have plans for the day." I was rambling. Stop rambling. "W-why are you calling?" A sudden idea seized me. "Please tell me you're not giving me my job back."

There was a pause. "You thought I fired you yesterday?"

Oh, Gabe hadn't told him yet. "No, not you."

"Not me? Then who?"

I was making this worse. "Why are you calling?" I asked instead. "Is there something you needed?"

"You're evading."

"So are you," I shot back. "And you called first. That makes my question have precedence."

"Well, I had a grand speech, but now it's gone." I heard him sigh in frustration. "I think I'd rather do this in person."

No. In-person was dangerous. My resolve would go up in smoke. "Whatever you have to say, you can say over the phone."

"All right, fine. I agree to your hundred grand demand."

My brain screeched to a halt. "What?"

"You said I didn't have skin in this game. Well, now I do. I'm agreeing to your demand."

I shoved the phone back to where it belonged. I did it without thinking. My brain screamed for space and that translated to hanging up on him. Oops.

I paced the small cabin. This had to be a dream. This wasn't happening. I did not just convince a powerful, wealthy, utterly gorgeous man, who could literally get any girl he wanted, to pay a nobody—me—one hundred grand for a stupid kiss.

I sank against the wall, falling to the floor, disgusted with myself. I was a swindler. That was the only way to explain this. It must be in my blood—criminality ingrained in me since birth. I couldn't get away from it no matter how hard I tried.

The phone trilled. I stared at it as if it was a ticking bomb, about to blow up. No way was I going to answer it.

It finally stopped. I pulled my knees up and plopped my head on them. It was official. I was a danger to everyone I knew. I should never leave this cabin.

A knock came at the door and I groaned. I had completely forgotten about that outing with Izzy. And I had promised her several times that I would not back out of it. If I didn't answer the door, that would mean I lied. And I didn't care if I was born a criminal—I was not going to start lying.

With a heavy sigh, I stood up, fixed my dress, then prepared for a long day with the chatty Izzy. But when I opened the door, I found David.

Two impulses burst on me: the need to run into his arms and the panic that would let me slam the door. My frozen brain couldn't decide so I just stood there. David, on the other hand, raised his eyebrows as his eyes traversed me. There was a hunger in his eyes—the same hunger Gabe had for Izzy.

"Wow," he breathed. "You look amazing."

Oh, no. I was wearing the flirty dress, charming him. I really was my dad.

That thought triggered my arm and it swung the door, but David stopped it with his hand, barging into the room.

I backed up hard, more to keep myself from running into his arms. "You can't be here."

"You hung up on me." He advanced toward me. I wanted him to catch me.

No, no, focus! "You can't pay me a hundred grand."

"Why not?"

"Because it's not right. I'm swindling you."

That stopped him, the confusion consuming his face. "You're doing this on purpose?"

If I lied, if I said yes, he'd be gone. He'd be safe. I would never see him again. But if I lied, wouldn't that make me like my dad anyway? It didn't matter. It was for his safety.

I opened my mouth, but nothing came out. Something inside me screamed against it; too many years of trying to be completely honest.

I covered my face. I couldn't lie, not even to save him. I was a horrible, horrible person.

David

I didn't know what was going on. I was trying to play her game but she kept changing the rules. She demanded money, but now refused it, claiming she was swindling me, and yet, she seemed terrified that she had succeeded. The way she was curled up, shoulders hunched up to her ears, hands over her face, made me want to pull her in and somehow calm her. But why claim she was swindling me? Was she lying? But which way? I didn't understand. Either she was messed up or this must be the best, most elaborate scheme ever in order to catch me.

I cleared my throat. "Lacy—"

"David?" Izzy called out.

I turned to see her at the door, staring at the two of us in confusion.

"What are you doing here?" Izzy continued.

Two minutes ago, the answer would have been easy, but now? I had no idea. "I—"

"He was leaving." Lacy had straightened up, the scared-little-girl image gone, replaced with a robotic version of herself. "Thanks for coming by, David."

I had no idea what had just happened, but I was not leaving until I got some answers. "Lacy—"

"Why should he leave?" Izzy cut in as she bounced into the room. "He can go with us. It will be so much fun!" She wrapped her arms around my waist and Lacy's and dragged us through the door before either of us could object. I expected Lacy to say something, but when she didn't, I remained quiet as well, letting Izzy pull us along on this outing she had planned. I soon learned she had a full day packed to the brim and she was the boss, which was ironic since I was her real boss. But I let her spit out the demands, such as Lacy sitting in the back while I sat in the front with

Izzy as she drove the rental car. Izzy seemed determined to keep us apart, and I let her get away with it.

It gave me time to think and to observe Lacy. She was so stiff. Izzy was the life of the party while Lacy seemed to be at a funeral. What was going on in that head of hers? Was she swindling me or not? And if she was, why tell me? Why not take the money and run? And if she wasn't swindling me, then why insist she was? I was giving her everything she wanted. What more did she want?

Unless... she didn't want *me*. I never really had asked if she was interested, just assumed based on her reactions to me. The way she had looked at me yesterday when I was about to kiss her, that certainly implied she liked me. But maybe it had only been a moment? I growled at myself. I really should be banned from attempting a romance. I was doing this all wrong.

I needed answers, but Izzy was in the way. How could I politely tell one employee that I wanted to sequester another employee in order to convince that one to let me date her?

"Ah!" Izzy cried. "I can hear the waterfall. We're close!" She grabbed my hand and tugged me to go faster along the path. I glanced at Lacy, but her eyes were centered on the leaf-strewn path. I hadn't once caught her looking in my direction.

"It's around the next bend," I announced, hoping to get Lacy to look up. She didn't.

"You've been here already?" Izzy asked with a slight pout. I wished Lacy would look at me like that.

"Many times. Came here every year with my parents. There are a bunch of waterfalls in this area, but this is one of the lesser-known ones."

Izzy giggled. "I know! I read it on the internet. Oh! There it is!"

We had rounded the bend and the waterfall was before us, cascading about ten feet. It wasn't the biggest in the area, but the pool was large enough for swimming. It was one of the reasons my family came here so often.

"We should jump in!" Izzy cried. "Look! There's a ledge up there. That would be perfect."

"No." Lacy's tone invited no argument. It was the first thing she had said all day.

Izzy looked at Lacy in shock.

"Lacy can't swim," I offered.

"Then she can stay here." Izzy grabbed my hand. "Come on!"

"You should check to see if it's deep enough first," I countered.

"Could you check for me?" She formed a pout. "Please?"

If Lacy had looked like that, I'd be in the water in seconds. But Izzy had no pull on me no matter how many times she batted her eyes at me. Then again, if Izzy was busy playing in the water, that would give me alone time with Lacy at last.

"Sure."

Izzy squealed and I couldn't help wondering what Lacy would be like if she was that happy. Right now, however, she was nothing close to happy, staying a very safe distance from the water's edge, her eyes on us as if she was sure we were heading to our deaths.

I strode to the pool. I wasn't prepared to get wet today, but it was hot enough that my shorts would dry off quickly. My shirt was cotton, though, so I pulled it off and wrapped my wallet and room key in it. Might as well have something remain dry.

There was an appreciative gasp behind me. A glance in that direction told me Izzy had been the gasper, her face of glee telling me how much she enjoyed me being shirtless. Lacy, on the other hand, was suddenly very interested in the ground around her feet. However, it wasn't hot enough to explain the flush on her face. I grinned. It was nice to see I could affect her as badly as she affected me.

I waded into the refreshingly cool water and swam to the area of inspection. "There's a rock here," I called out, tapping it with my sandal, "but if you aim for this spot," I pointed to a wide, deep area, "you should be fine." I returned to the shallow shore and Izzy had her hands around my arm in seconds.

"You have to show me up there!" She pointed to the ledge. "That way, I won't get confused."

I hesitated. The whole point of the inspection was for Izzy to go away so I could talk to Lacy. But Izzy had a point. Me pointing in the water where the safe spot to land was not as effective as pointing while up on the ledge. After Izzy jumped, then I could pester Lacy for answers.

"All right." I followed Izzy up to the protruding ledge. Once up there, I pointed to the spot. "Right there and you should be fine."

But Izzy's gaze was on Lacy, who stared up at us. "The poor thing."

I raised an eyebrow. "Because she can't swim?"

"No, because she got fired."

I frowned. Lacy had mentioned that, too. "Who fired her?"

"Gabe."

"What? Why? When?"

"Yesterday at the resort. Lacy's been giving him grief for ages and he had had it. She's really not a trustworthy person. I've been trying for ages to be her friend, but she and Sarah, her roommate, are very closed off. But, it's not really much of a surprise, considering what Gabe learned."

I didn't like the sound of this. "What did Gabe learn?"

Izzy shrugged. "That she and Sarah are thieves."

I frowned. Had Gabe told Izzy about the stolen millions? He shouldn't have done that, if so. But why had Gabe included Sarah? "Do you know Sarah?"

She nodded. "I know them both, and Gabe is right. Those two like to act poor but you should see how much Sarah spends. No idea where she gets the money." Izzy clucked her tongue. "Lacy, though, she gets men to spend for her instead. She loves being showered with money. It's a good thing you're too smart for her tricks." Izzy suddenly brightened. "Here I go!" And then she jumped, screaming all the way down before ending in a big splash.

Chapter 24

Lacy

I WOULD NEVER CLAIM to be a swimming expert, but by all *my* counts, Izzy could swim. She had popped up immediately, then splashed around without hesitation and called for David to jump in as well. He, however, had already descended, heading straight for me.

I gulped. I had been dreading this moment. While I had never enjoyed being with Izzy, she had been useful in keeping David engaged and away from me. She had been a lot clingier than I had expected, but then, she had just been dumped. Maybe she had hoped David could fill the hole in her heart. Unfortunately, he seemed to only have eyes for me. My powers of swindling were too strong.

"Let's walk," he said. It wasn't an invitation.

"There's no trail." I indicated the maze of trees before us. "We could get lost."

"I know this area very well." He put a hand on the small of my back to propel me forward, but the touch sent electricity up my spine. And he was still shirtless. I didn't know where to look with all that muscle on display.

"How long have you known Izzy?" David asked, still propelling me into the maze of trees, the roar of the waterfall fading behind us.

"N-not very long." It was hard to concentrate with his hand at my back and his hulking chest muscles beside me. "She started working with Sarah over a year ago."

"How long have you known Sarah?"

"W-why are we talking about Sarah?"

His hand moved to my arm as he turned me to face him. "Why do you always avoid talking about her?" That was his I-think-you're-lying tone.

"She's a good friend. My only friend. I don't want her caught up in this mess I'm in."

He eyed me. "What if I have reason to believe she is involved?"

I pulled away from him. "She's not. She's a good person. If you want to hate someone, hate me, but leave her out of this."

He raised an eyebrow. "First you demand money, then claim you're swindling me, and now I'm supposed to hate you?"

I glared at him. "You're acting like that doesn't make sense."

"It doesn't."

"Yes, it does. I'm doing terrible things, so hate me for them."

He narrowed his eyes. "Do you hate *me*?"

"What? No."

"Do you *like* me?"

That was a dangerous question. "I can't answer that."

He stepped toward me. "Why not?"

I took a step backward. "It's not appropriate."

He grinned. "So you do like me."

"I didn't say that."

"Lacy, if you are trying to swindle me, you should at least pretend to like me."

"I'm not trying to swindle you."

"Then why are you claiming you are?" he shot back.

"Because you're threatening to pay me a hundred grand."

"You demanded it."

I threw up my hands. "I didn't think you'd accept it!"

"Why not? You feared I wouldn't have enough money?"

"This was never about your money. This is about the fact that you can't like me."

"And why can't I like you?" He stepped closer.

My back hit a tree. I couldn't back up farther. "B-because I'm making you like me."

He put a hand on the tree next to my ear and leaned toward me. "And that's bad because..."

The intensity in his eyes was making my knees weak. I wrapped my hands around the tree behind me so they wouldn't end around his neck. "Because that's what my dad did."

David

Things were starting to finally make sense. She'd watched her dad use people her whole life and was terrified she was becoming him.

"You didn't dupe me into liking you, if that's what you're saying," I said.

She shook her head. "That has to be the only explanation. There's no other reason for your interest."

I wanted to shake her. Did she really have such a poor opinion of herself?

"Do you know what I first thought when I saw you?" I asked.

"Hapless female by herself," she muttered, her eyes on anything but me, "looking lonely while gazing out at the ocean."

"Hardly. You were in the line to get on the ship."

Her eyes shot to mine. "T-the line?"

I nodded. "Josh was doing his grand entrance, remember? And out of that whole crowd, you were the only one not watching him." I swept a stray curl from her forehead. "And I found myself staring. At you. No one else. Just you. And when I saw you again on the deck, I told Josh he could flirt with any girl, but not you. You, he had to leave alone."

Her eyes were wide. "Why?"

"Because"—I leaned closer, her lips tantalizing close—"there is something about you"—I dug my hand into her hair again, tilting her head up—"that I. Can't. Get. Enough. Of."

My lips found hers. My blood raced; the world faded away. It was just me and her and I couldn't get enough. I had kissed before, but it never felt like this, as though my whole body was on fire.

My phone vibrated. I ignored it. I didn't care if it was an important message or the alarm telling me to be back at the ship. Nothing was tearing me from this girl.

But she pulled her lips from mine. "Your phone.

I wanted to curse the thing. "It's not important."

"But Izzy—"

Oh, yeah. We'd left her alone at the waterfall. With a sigh, I raised my head, but I kept a firm hand around her waist, keeping her close. Pulling out my phone, I checked what had come in. Then frowned.

"What is it?" she asked.

"An email from my investigators."

"They found out who's framing me?"

"I don't know." I reluctantly let her go so I could read it. The email was long but a quick scan made the blood inside me freeze. They had finally found someone who had spent the stolen millions. And it was Sarah, Lacy's roommate. Her only friend. Her confidant.

Lacy had channeled the money to Sarah, the email concluded. While Sarah had never been charged with a crime, she had family who had a history of stealing. Lacy and Sarah were two peas in a pod, the email claimed, both experienced in the art of theft.

The world seemed to spin. What had Izzy said? The two acted poor but were anything but that.

I pushed away from Lacy. I needed air. My lungs suddenly couldn't get enough. My head spun. I couldn't see straight. Had everything been a lie? Lacy was so confusing. She was hot and cold, open but closed, frank but evasive. Everything inside me screamed Lacy must be innocent, but my emotions were tainted. I had to follow facts—follow the evidence.

And they all pointed to Lacy.

Lacy

I didn't know what was going on, but whatever David had read on his phone, it had devastated him.

"What happened?" I asked.

"Sarah. Do you trust her?" he barked.

I backed up. "Why are we talking about Sarah again?"

That was the wrong thing to say. I could tell by the anger flaring in his eyes. "Answer the question, Lacy."

"Yes. She's my best friend."

"And is she poor like you?"

I didn't understand where this was going. "Why are you asking?"

"Stop evading and answer it."

There could only be one reason he was so interested in Sarah all of a sudden. "Sarah is not involved in this mess."

"Then explain how Sarah has spent over a million dollars in the past two months."

I gasped. "That's not true. That can't be true."

"She opened a new card two months ago under a false name. According to this," he waved his phone, "that's something you used to do a lot with your dad. So either you lied and she *is* involved, or you're using her to hide spending the millions you stole from me."

"No, this is all wrong. You know someone is framing me."

"You saying it's Sarah?"

I shook my head. It couldn't be Sarah. Or could it? When she had walked in that day, she had wanted to know if I would help her abscond with a million dollars. What if that hadn't been rhetorical like she had claimed? What if she really had been the one stealing all those millions?

But why would she frame me? We were friends! *Best* friends!

"Well?" David demanded.

"This doesn't make sense," I countered. "She doesn't have the access or the knowledge. She doesn't even know how to forge a signature!"

"But you do."

I swallowed hard. My only saving grace had been my lack of spending. But Sarah had just sunk that hope. "I didn't do it."

His stare was unreadable, but the bulging muscle in his jaw was loud enough. "I think you need a lawyer," he stated in low voice. Then he turned and walked away.

I just stood there, my brain still reeling, unable to process what had happened. David insisting he cared for me. That he couldn't get enough. And his kiss. It was like my world had exploded. But now he was gone, claiming I was the thief, the bad guy, the villain.

No, that Sarah was the thief. That I had fed her the money. But neither was true. None of it was true!

I covered my face. How did this happen? Who would have created such an elaborate plan to frame me? And why me? I didn't do anything!

I threw my hands down in frustration, then stomped after David. Except I didn't know where he had gone. I whirled around, scanning my surroundings. The trees looked all the same, the area quiet, devoid of useful sound to tell me where to go. Which way had David walked? Which way had we come?

I pressed against the tree, fear clawing at my stomach.

I was lost.

Chapter 25

David

I stomped into the clearing of the waterfall, wanting to punch anything that moved. Unfortunately, the first thing that moved was Izzy. Definitely couldn't do that.

"You guys left me all alone!" She bounded up to me. "Why did you do that? Where's Lacy? Did she get lost again?"

I muttered under my breath. I had left Lacy all by herself in an unknown forest. Despite everything, I couldn't leave her like that. "I'll get her."

"No." Izzy grabbed my arm. "You look like you need air. Go back to the car. I'll get Lacy."

"You sure?"

"Don't worry about a thing. In fact, you can walk down the road. We'll pick you up when you've cooled off."

Izzy was such a nice girl. "Thanks." I headed for the trail, then stopped. "Actually, don't wait for me. I'll get my own ride back to the ship."

"But it's getting dark!"

"I know my way around here." I waved at her. "Make sure you get yourselves to the ship on time."

She waved back. "Don't worry, we will!"

"Good." I headed down a different trail. It would take longer, but it should give me the time to cool off and get my head back on.

Lacy

"Lacy!" Izzy's voice called out, echoing through the trees.

I had never been so happy to hear her voice in my life. "I'm over here!" I rushed toward Izzy when she called out again, then hugged her hard. "I'm so glad you found me!"

Izzy laughed. "What are friends for?"

Ooo, ouch. She'd done a lot for me lately but I still kept her at arm's length. "Sorry I haven't been very nice to you."

"Don't worry about it." She linked her arm through mine and led the way. "I'm just glad that you finally trust me."

I grimaced. "It wasn't that I didn't trust you. We just have... different priorities."

"Isn't that the truth!" Izzy giggled. "But I really do wish we had gone shopping at least once together. Would have saved so much time."

Something in her tone made me tense. Something about shopping. Hadn't every single time Izzy had seen me, she had pressed me to go shopping? I had never gone, but Sarah had. Several times. And it was Sarah who had spent millions.

With Izzy.

A cold pit formed in my stomach. "Izzy—"

"I saw David," she announced airily, but there was a steel edge to her tone. "He looked pretty upset. But you would have been proud. He offered to come and find you when I pointed out he had left you behind. Such a good guy, going to save the helpless, lost Lacy. You really are good with men."

I tried to wiggle my arm free from her but she tightened her hold. "Dear Lacy," she continued in that overly sweet tone she had always used on me, the one that had subconsciously irritated me, "don't forget you have a terrible sense of direction. Do you really want to try getting out of here by yourself? You could be lost for days." She flashed me a grin, but it was her eyes that gave me chills.

"You're the one who's framing me."

She giggled as if I had told the funniest joke. "Why ever would I do something like that to a friend? To such a nice, caring"—her nails dug into my arm—"*friend*, huh, Amy?"

Amy. My real name. The blood drained from my face.

"You told me," Izzy continued, pulling me up an incline, "that your father would fix everything, remember? And I let you introduce your father to my parents. Don't you remember, Amy, dear? But you must remember since you picked my older sister's name as your new one."

Lacy and Elizabeth. The two girls of the family I had helped destroy. I couldn't seem to swallow. There was no more liquid in my mouth. "I-I never meant—"

"I always wondered," she continued, still in that sweet, happy tone, "if you thought of us. If you were around when we lost our home, when my parents divorced, or when my dad attempted suicide not once, but twice. But, that was silly, wasn't it? Because we were just a checkmark"—she dug her nails deeper into my skin, her chilled smile turning into a snarl—"on your long list of conquests, weren't we?"

"T-that's not true. I took Lacy's name because I regretted—"

She giggled again. I was going to be haunted by that sound for the rest of my life, I was sure of it. "You're so funny with your lies. So serious when you deliver them. But we both know you have no soul in you." We stepped out of the foliage and I stiffened. Water roared to my right, spitting out over an edge and descending into a vast pool below—and only four feet of ledge between me and that deep pool.

"In the mood for a swim, Amy dear?"

I clutched the hand wrapped around my arm, my other hand wrapping around a branch hanging overhead while my feet dug in as hard as they could into the soft soil. "Please don't!"

"Don't be so scared, Lacy. I'm your friend, remember?" She wrapped an arm around my waist and tugged me forward. "And friends would never purposefully harm someone, right?"

Panic surged through me. I grabbed her arm and ripped it from my waist, then shoved her as hard as I could. She teetered backward, but in the direction I needed to go. Stupid! I should have shoved her toward the ledge!

I bolted anyway, but she caught my arm. The momentum of my speed caused us to spin—and she swung me right into a tree. Pain exploded in my shoulder and head as they connected with the tree. Black spots sprouted in my vision. I blinked hard, trying to clear them. Where was the ledge? I could not afford to get lost and go the wrong way!

But hands abruptly shoved me forward. I fell, then yelped. The ledge was just inches away.

"Help!" I screamed.

Izzy just laughed, a heavy branch now in her hands. "You think your precious David is going to save you? He's gone, sweetie. Said he would find his own way home, so it's just you and me and this lovely waterfall that will drown any of your pitiful screams."

"Izzy, please!"

"Oh, are you begging me now? But did you let my family do that?" She leveled the branch at me. "You know, if you had just gone shopping with me, we wouldn't be here. I had it all planned out. But no, I had to resort to your awful roommate, Sarah. And she wouldn't even buy the expensive stuff. I had to do all that. But it should still have worked. You were supposed to walk off the ship in handcuffs on Key West. I had sweetened Gabe up, dropping all the little details needed so he would lay out the proof to David. It was perfect. But then you"—she wagged the branch at me—"you had to sink your claws into David."

I shook my head. "I didn't—"

"I saw you that first day at the meeting," she spat. "You cared only about talking with David, to win him over."

"No—"

"And you did. You got him to pay for the snorkeling activity, to take you around as your tour guide. I saw how besotted he became with you. I knew if I let this continue, you were going to get away scot-free. Just like you did when your dad got caught. They only put you away for two years. A measly two years for the *lifetime* of pain you gave to me and my family."

"Izzy, please. I was young and stupid. I didn't mean to hurt you."

"Yes, yes, just like how I don't mean to hurt you right now." She shoved the branch at me. I grabbed it, clutching for dear life.

"If you push me over, you're coming with me," I shot at her.

She smiled like a lion at its prey. "But I can swim, Amy dear. But don't worry. I'll save you. Like how you saved my family." She shoved hard, pushing me over. I clawed at the branch as if it would magically make me stop falling. Izzy had gone over, too, but no terror lit up her face. No, that was only on mine.

We hit the water with a smack, then chilly liquid swallowed me whole. Down, down I went. I kicked. I flapped. I screamed. Bubbles came out.

Bubbles. Air. What had David said?

Air in my lungs made me float.

I clamped my mouth shut. *Please float.* I curled into a ball. *Please float.* My lungs hurt. *Please, please float.* Did I have enough air? *Please float!*

Something weird hit my back. Nothing solid. Just a different sensation, like it was being tickled by air.

Air!

I lunged upward and found glorious, life-saving air. I gulped it, sucking in as much as possible. But the water crashed around me again. The waterfall churned the water, grasping at me. I sank back into the murky depths.

I held my breath again and curled into a ball. Back to the surface I floated, up into the air I gasped. Where was Izzy? Was she really going to leave me here to drown? I couldn't see her. I couldn't see anyone—or anything. Just water. All around me. I repeated holding my breath, then clawing for air, but I sucked in less air each time. I was tiring. I couldn't do this forever. I flapped and kicked again. There had to be a way to stay on the surface or to move or something, but nothing I did seemed to work.

Land had to be close by. Safety was only feet away. I had to swim! David had mention floating on my back, but I couldn't figure out the process. The waterfall made the water too choppy. And my strength was leaving me. I was exhausted.

I gasped for air again, but water came in instead. I coughed, spewing it out, but only more water came in. Oh no. No, please no. If no more air, then no more floating.

I clawed at the water as I sunk under. I kicked as hard as I could. But nothing worked.

I was dead.

Chapter 26

David

I MUTTERED HOTLY AS I stormed back toward the waterfall. I had forgotten my shirt and my wallet. More proof that I didn't have my head on straight. I glanced around for fear of seeing Lacy or Izzy, but no one was in the area. It had been a while—they should already be in the car, heading to the ship. With relief, I headed for where my shirt lay on a bush. But something caught my eye. Someone was in the water. A girl. And she was drowning.

Lacy.

I hadn't been a lifeguard in years, but all the training rushed back. The worst thing to do was to dive in and save her by myself. Her panic would make her latch onto me and, with her lacking air, she'd be a dead weight, dragging us both under. But I had no floating device, no rope, nothing to throw out to her. And if I didn't act fast, she was never going to be seen again.

There had been a huge rock near where she was, hadn't there? I had found it when checking for Izzy's jump. That would have to be what I used.

I rushed into the water, swimming hard. Where was that rock? Lacy's head was underwater now; I could only see her hands, her fingers outstretched as if they could breathe for her. Where was that stupid rock? Never mind—she wasn't going to last another second.

I dove under, reaching for her. My hand grasped silky hair. That was enough. I grabbed a handful and pulled. Her body jerked toward me. I needed to get her head above water but not let her cling to me or we'd both drown. I took a deep breath, then gripped the back of her head and shoved it upward, causing me to go under. The muscles of her neck moved under my fingers. That felt like coughing. Good. She was alive.

Her body twisted—no doubt trying to grab onto me. Keeping her as far away from me as possible but her head still above the water, I kicked my legs hard to push myself back up. Her moves became frantic and I was losing my grip on the back of her head. If she kept this up, she was going to go under again.

Praying this didn't kill us both, I yanked her toward me, then hooked an elbow under her chin to keep her head up and hissed, "I got you, but don't grab on to me or we both drown!"

Lacy

David's voice rang in my head like a trumpet. Everything inside me relaxed at once. I had no idea where he had come from but it didn't matter. He was here. I was safe.

"I'm going to drag you to the shore," David hissed in my ear, "Just relax and don't move."

My lungs hurt, my breathing gurgled. I didn't know if words could come out so I tried to nod instead. With his arm around my throat, he should have sensed the movement. The waterfall still roared somewhere nearby and the cold water clutched at my dress, dragging me down. My breath came shorter, the gurgling sound increasing. My lungs felt like a fire was within them—every breath hurt. I needed to cough but didn't dare do it for fear it might kill us both. Were we moving? I couldn't tell. The water was too choppy. It was all around. It was never-ending.

"Put your feet down," David commanded.

What? Already? I stretched out my feet for the glorious ground, but couldn't seem to reach it. Where was it?

"I—" The second I tried to speak, I coughed. Hard. Water came out.

David wrapped his arms around me and hefted me out of the water. I tried to cling to his shirt but discovered only bare skin, so I gripped his neck. And I coughed. Coughed all over his shirtless chest. Somewhere, in some part of my mind, I was mortified. But it was overwhelmed with the intense need to breathe.

He put me down and my feet felt sand—my shoes were gone. The stupid water ate them. My knees buckled, but David clasped two hands around my shoulders, keeping me up as I coughed.

"Are you okay?" David barked once my coughing subsided.

I nodded. My lungs still hurt—I didn't want to try to talk.

"Why you were in the water?" He shook my shoulders. "What were you thinking? You know you can't swim!"

He was mad at me? Why was he mad? I had just nearly drowned!

Suddenly he crushed me to him, hugging me so hard, I couldn't breathe again. But I had no strength to fight. Oh well. Death by hugging was more enjoyable than death by drowning.

"Don't ever do that again!" he hissed into my ear.

I agreed wholeheartedly to that, but nothing came out of my mouth. Because he was still crushing me with his big, strong arms. He really was going to kill me by hugging.

I squirmed, mainly for him to let up slightly, but he immediately pulled me away from him, propping me up on my feet. I had no strength, though. It was all gone, sucked dry by the water. So he picked me up, cradling me in his arms.

"We've got to find Izzy," he announced, marching forward.

"No!" It shot out of my mouth like a rising phoenix from my lungs. "No!" I squirmed against his arms, digging my nails into his chest. I'd rather he tossed me back in the water than get me anywhere near Izzy.

He stopped and propped me in a way so he could search my face. "We have to get you to a doctor. Izzy has a car—"

"No!" Ugh, it hurt to talk, but it was either that or Izzy killing us both. "She pushed me!"

His eyes shot wide open. "*Izzy* did this? Why?"

"Lacy. Elizabeth," I rasped, but the pain was subsiding with each word. "The framing, everything. It's revenge for when I was Amy."

David

I stared at Lacy. "Izzy?" She had seemed so nice. And Gabe was besotted with her. "Are you sure? Do you have proof?"

Pain flashed in her eyes. "You don't... believe me?"

I blew out my breath. My gut said I should, but less than twenty minutes ago, I had solid proof Lacy had been the one orchestrating all of this. Was it possible Lacy could have faked the drowning so I'd trust her again?

No, she had no idea I was coming back. And she certainly was drowning. If I had shown up one minute later, she would have been dead. Someone as smart as Lacy wouldn't be stupid enough to risk death on the off chance I'd make it in time to rescue her.

"I want to believe you," I said. "I swear I do. It's just... the facts don't line up and I need to follow facts."

"The car," Lacy rasped. "I bet the car is gone. Would that be proof?"

I moved at once, carrying Lacy down the trail. Izzy had promised to retrieve Lacy, and she knew Lacy got lost easily. There was no way a nice girl like Izzy would leave without making sure Lacy was in the car.

The second I saw the empty car lot, I stopped. I didn't care if Izzy was the thief or not—the fact that she had left Lacy to die boiled my blood.

"Believe me now?" Lacy asked.

I crushed her to me. "I'm sorry. I just... everything pointed to you. I didn't know what to think."

"It's okay. I know my past... isn't good."

"You said she pushed you, right?"

"Yes."

"I need to put you down."

"O-okay."

I deposited her on a pile of rocks, then pulled out my phone. It was wet from my swim, but it was top-of-the-line waterproof. Dialing a number, I soon had one of my favorite car rental agencies on the line. The instant they learned my name, they rained down promises, insisting they would have a car driven to me within twenty minutes. Thanking them, I hung up, then sat down next to Lacy.

"Tell me everything you know."

She dictated the long saga, her body drooping the more she went on. "So, in a way," she added, "I deserved this."

"Listen." I made her face me. "*No one* deserves to be left to drown; I don't care what they've done in their lives. And you already paid—you went to jail, then changed your whole life."

"Yeah, but my web of lies will always haunt me."

"Not for me." I covered her hand with mine. "I know I haven't been the best at it, but I swear, from now on, you have my trust."

She nodded numbly. "But I hurt Izzy so badly."

"I hurt you, too, didn't I? I condemned you for a crime you didn't commit and then I left you alone with someone who intended you harm. You think I should drown for that?"

"No."

I squeezed her hand. "Then stop thinking you deserved any of this. Both you and Izzy went through something traumatic. You both blindly trusted someone. But *you* chose to not let it consume you. She did not."

She was silent for a moment. "How did you find me? Izzy claimed you had left."

"I had, but I'd forgotten my shirt. Which," I pointed to my bare chest, "I did again, apparently."

"Yeah, I noticed." She averted her eyes, the flush apparent across her cheeks again.

I grinned. "Like it, huh?"

She shot me a glare. "Really? You're going to ask that now?"

"Sorry. I've always been bad at saying the right things at the right time."

"My hair's a mess, anyway," she muttered, patting it. "I bet I look awful."

I chuckled. "Your hair is dangerous."

She eyed me. "Why?"

"Because, every time I touch it"—I pushed several wet strands from her face—"I just want to kiss you." I tugged her a little closer to me. She didn't resist. "You could have the craziest hair"—I threaded my fingers into her hair, cupping her head—"and I'd still have trouble keeping my eyes off of you."

"Keep talking," she breathed.

"Don't want to talk..." My lips brushed hers. They trembled at my touch. I pulled her closer, hungry for everything about her. But the low growl of an engine interrupted us as the rental car pulled into the parking lot. They had shown up right on time as promised. It was the first time I had ever wished they had been late.

I helped Lacy to her feet. She wobbled, but at least she remained standing instead of buckling earlier.

"I really need to get my shirt," I said as I helped her toward the car.

"No, please don't."

I grinned. "So you *do* like me shirtless."

"I like you." She leaned against me, her head on my chest. "And I don't want to be alone."

"The driver won't hurt you."

"He's not as cute as you."

I laughed and wrapped my arms around her. "Are you making me choose between my shirt and you?"

"Do I win?"

"Yes," I growled and kissed the top of her head. "I'll send the driver to get the shirt and my wallet."

"He'll think you're weird."

"I don't think he'll care once he gets my fat tip." I helped her into the backseat, then directed the request to the driver before climbing in myself and sitting next to Lacy. She immediately snuggled into me and I put my arm around her, resisting the urge to kiss her again. We might be alone now, but I had a feeling neither of us would notice when the driver returned.

Chapter 27

Lacy

WITH DAVID'S SHIRT BACK on, I nestled into his side as the car headed for the dock. I felt completely safe and relaxed in his arms, but a small fear kept chirping.

"I don't want to see Izzy, please," I finally voiced.

"Yeah," he murmured against my hair. "I don't either. I think I'd end up strangling her or something."

"We'll have to hide in our cabins, then."

"Mmm... how about we miss the ship?"

I looked up at him. "What?"

"It's heading back to Miami with a whole boring day at sea. You won't miss much, I promise."

"But, my clothes!"

"I'll send my butler to gather them. He'll have them with my stuff when they dock."

"Yeah, but that means I'm stuck in this dress for two days."

"It's a very pretty dress."

"Not after two days," I muttered.

He laughed. "I'll buy you a new wardrobe then."

"You cannot shower me with money."

"I'm not. I owe you two hundred grand for two kisses."

I poked him in his chest. "I wasn't serious about that."

He kissed the top of my head. "I was."

"Then I'm going to have to ban you from kissing me." I pulled away from him. He laughed and tugged me toward him but I resisted. "I don't want anyone thinking that I'm with you for the money."

"Okay, valid point. How about this: The money is an advance from your pay."

I scoffed. "I don't earn a hundred grand even in a year. Also, I don't want to work under Gabe anymore."

"You won't be seeing him."

I eyed him. "You're firing him?"

He shook his head. "I've been needing a really smart tech support manager who can make up macros on the spot when I need them."

Joy shot through me. "You mean—"

"The job is yours if you don't mind relocating to New York City. And yes, it will pay a lot more than your old job. I also have an empty company condo you can use until you can find your own place in the city."

I hesitated. "Does this position require a secretary or any clerks?"

He raised an eyebrow. "I guess it could?"

"Could I suggest Sarah for that spot?"

He frowned. "Wasn't Sarah helping Izzy?"

"No, Izzy was using her. She told me herself."

"Okay, but are you sure you can trust Sarah?"

"Yes," I said. "She's like me. Her only brother is in jail so we're basically family for each other. I can't leave her behind. She has no one else and she was there for me when I needed someone."

"What did she do for you?"

"She got me this job. The first one, not the one you're offering now."

"Ah," he said. "But how did she get the job working for my company in the first place?"

"You have a program where you offer a temporary job for battered women. She proved her worth and was given a permanent one."

"Wait, are you saying she used to get *hit*?"

I shrugged. "Like I said, she has no one good in her life except me."

"All right. If you think she'll do a good job, she can come, too."

"Then I accept." I re-snuggled into his side. "What about Izzy?"

"She is *not* coming."

I laughed. "You know that is not what I meant."

"I'll make some calls. She should be getting off in cuffs when the ship docks in Miami. You won't have to worry about her for a long time."

"Mmm," I murmured. "Your dad will be happy, too. You caught the thief."

"I'm just happy I caught the *right* thief." He threaded his fingers through my hair, sending currents of giddiness through me.

"Me, too." I let out a peaceful sigh. "Though, there is one thing I still want."

"Name it."

"I really, really, really want to learn how to swim."

He gave my shoulders a squeeze. "I wholeheartedly agree."

David

The first call I made was to Josh.

"I have good news," I began. "I will not be blaming you for the dissolved relationship between Gabe and Izzy."

"You better," Josh grumbled. "I haven't been near Izzy all day! And Gabe's been moping about, trying to find her. Apparently, she ditched him today and he has no idea why. He insists they parted on good terms yesterday. I bet she found someone better."

"There's a long story to this," I began, "but I want to know if Izzy made it back to the ship. Can you find that out for me?"

"Can't you ask the butler to do that?"

"I'm not on the ship."

"What? Why? Where are you? I haven't seen you all day. Are you okay?"

"I'm fine. Lacy and I are going to fly back."

"Oh ho! So the suite is now mine? Yes!"

I rolled my eyes. "No throwing my stuff out."

Josh laughed. "I'm sure there's a closet they can find to store it in."

"Josh," I warned.

"Don't worry. I'll make sure all your boring stuff is delivered to your penthouse. You should probably arrange for flowers to be sent to your abandoned laptop. I'm sure it's weeping right now."

"Very funny, Josh."

"I take it I should direct the butler to collect Lacy's, too?"

"That would be appreciated, yes."

"So, you paying the hundred grand a kiss?"

"It's gone up. A lot."

"You don't sound mad about that."

"Let's just say I can see why you'd blow a couple million on a girl."

"What is this? David Wellington is willingly spending money? I'm glad I don't have your dad's heart. I'd be suffering an attack right now."

"Yeah, well, I still have to tell my parents about this."

"Wait a couple of weeks. Relationships never last longer than that."

"For you, maybe. I'm hoping this won't be the case."

"Wow, the love bug really does bite deep for you. Don't spread it to me."

I laughed. "I've got to make some other calls but let me know about Izzy."

"Will do."

My next call was to my sister. I had to keep my phone a foot away while Jane squealed in delight.

"Don't tell Mom and Dad yet," I said. "I'd like to warm them up to this."

"I'll help with the warming."

"Thanks. I'll need it."

The following calls were to my investigating team, my attorneys, and to one of my favorite resorts. My dad used to talk about how he courted my mom and I had the perfect evening planned out.

Lacy

David had a medical team waiting for us when we arrived at a huge resort. Once the medics checked me over and found nothing to be concerned about, the employees showed us to a secluded wing where I could have my pick of any of the large suites with floor-to-ceiling windows facing the ocean. David took the one next to mine and then let me use his phone to make a call.

"I can't believe it!" Sarah cried once I gave her the short version of everything that had happened. "It was Izzy this *whole* time?"

"Yeah. She was a fake friend for the both of us."

"You know, I always had this sense she was trying to use me. But I had no idea what she could get out of me so I ignored the feeling. Sarah, I'm so sorry—"

"It's not your fault."

"But I was the one that went shopping with her. If I hadn't—"

"I'm sure she would have found another way to ensnare me."

"And then you wouldn't have met David!"

I laughed. "That's one way to look at it."

Sarah sighed as if in dreamland. "I can't believe how this ended up so well. And now he's going to whisk you away to a castle somewhere."

"We're only at a resort. Besides, he doesn't live in a castle."

"Then he should buy one. You deserve a princess ending."

"I don't need a castle," I countered with a laugh. "And I don't need him spending any money on me."

But that statement turned out to be wrong since I still needed a new wardrobe and had no purse or money. David ended up handing me his credit card to shop for some clothes at the overly expensive shop in the resort. When I came back with the cheapest outfit, he then ordered a bunch of clothes in my size to be brought up—with the request that the prices be hidden from me.

"I thought I told you no showering money on me," I accused him as we sat on a beach reserved just for us, a dinner picnic spread out. Torches flickered around us, casting a warm glow. I was dressed in red again—a sundress that I hoped wasn't outrageously expensive—but it had lit up David's eyes when I had tried it on, so I kept it.

"I'm doing no such thing," he countered with a grin. "A friend of mine owns this and he owes me a favor. You just happened to be along when I cashed in."

I shook my head, trying hard not to grin. "You're going to keep making up excuses, aren't you?"

"What can I say?" He twirled his fingers into my hair. "You stole my heart."

"So is this jail?" I snuck my arms around his neck. "'Cause if it is, give me twenty years at least."

He grinned, leaning in. "No, this crime is worth at least a lifetime."

"Deal."

The End

Author's Note

Aren't David and Lacy adorable? I might be biased, but I think so! I'd love to hear your thoughts whether you agree or not so go and leave me a review! It doesn't have to be anything fancy, just a quick note saying whether or not you liked the book. As an independent author, every review really helps me out. And I'd love to hear your thoughts!

Also, I had an epilogue planned. A short one. But then it developed a plot... and is no longer short. Oops! But now you get even more David and Lacy in the sequel novella as he introduces her to his formidable parents and you can get it for free! Just hop over and nab it at https://bit.ly/3t6rgls.

Next up is Sarah's story in *Saving My Billionaire Protector*. Here's the synopsis:

Sarah's got health problems, can't handle stress, and has a nasty past. No man is going to want to deal with that. So she's sworn them all off. She's shy anyway so it wasn't like she had much of a chance in the first place.

But then she meets tall, brawny, and billionaire Mark.

And gets kidnapped with him.

Mark wasn't expecting to get kidnapped. But neither did he expect to lose his heart to the gorgeous gal who got roped into his mess. But she pushes him away even though he's the only guy on the boat that doesn't want her dead. If he wants to win her heart, he has to prove himself to her as well as save themselves from the thugs.

But forced proximity brings out a lot of secrets. And Sarah has some big ones. Will he be able to handle them?

Enjoy this fast-pace, suspenseful, clean romance! Buy it now or read on for a sneak peek!

Sneak Peek of Saving My Billionaire Protector

Chapter One: Sarah

I HAD THE WORST luck on the planet.

I glared at the frail woman in the cracked mirror of this dismal public bathroom. The heat of the day had caused my long, black hair to plaster itself to the sides of my face, and my long-sleeve turtleneck clung to my thin, petite body in unattractive ways. Add the fact that I had limped my way to this bathroom, and it was a wonder I didn't have 'weak, hideous female' flashing above me.

And yet, the cute guy in the café couldn't keep his eyes off me.

That was not a good thing. Because cute guys normally didn't look at me. At all. Which meant this was new. And I didn't handle new things well. They stressed me out.

And stress could kill me. Literally.

I pushed back my hair. Along my right temple, a rash crawled beyond the hairline, the angry red bumps crowned with crusty flakes of white. And it itched, like pinpoints of fire, begging me to scratch and make it worse; maybe even bleed. That itch spread over my entire scalp, and it was taking all of my willpower to not give in.

Dabbing medicinal lotion onto my forehead, I took two deep breaths. Stress made the rash grow. Which was why I tried to live a life with the least amount of stress. So, that meant no cute guys and definitely no spontaneity. Except, what did I decide to do today?

Venture into a gang-infested neighborhood.

Yeah, I had lost my brain. Or maybe the rash had finally seeped into my skull and poisoned it. Speaking of the rash, it had developed on my feet, too. That was why I had ventured into this dingy café bathroom. It hurt too much to walk. So, now I was stranded in a bad neighborhood with a really cute guy sitting out there who, with my luck, was probably a gangster judging by his confident smile, bulging muscles, and designer clothing. No one else would be stupid enough to flaunt wealth in this neighborhood. Which meant I was in a terrible scenario for someone who couldn't stress out.

I wiggled my toes, the closest I'd dare get to scratching the rash. I had already lathered the medicine over my feet—after covering the not-clean toilet seat with an obscene amount of toilet paper—and while it, thankfully, eased the itch, the pain still roared.

Taking another deep breath, I counted to four, then let it out slowly, counting to four once more. A breathing exercise I resorted to when desperate. I needed to think reasonably, not stupidly. Despite the pain, I could walk a little. Okay, more like hobble, but it would count as movement. Still, I didn't want to catch the cute guy's attention again. He had smiled at me as if the lone, limping female walking into his café was the best thing that had happened to him all day. Yeah, not a good sign. Not in this neighborhood.

If I snuck out the back, the closest bus stop was fifteen minutes away, however. I should know since I had just walked from it. And I had another ten minutes of walking before I reached the reason that had brought me to this dangerous neighborhood in the first place.

I eyed myself, trying to make the decision. Six months ago, it would have been obvious: never do anything stressful. It was a good motto. My rash had reduced in size, disappearing from everywhere but my scalp. Ever since my diagnosis seven years ago, I had managed to keep my auto-immune disease in check and not have to fear dying at any moment.

But then Lacy met David.

Lacy was my best friend and roommate. Like me, her growing-up years had been rough; she had a lot of baggage and needed to lay low. We were two peas in a pod, both trying to survive in a world where the odds were stacked against us.

Until the odds abruptly lined up perfectly in Lacy's favor almost a year ago. Now she had the perfect life: a job she loved, people who accepted her despite her flaws, and a fairytale romance with a handsome billionaire.

Why couldn't I get such luck?

Instead, I would be all alone. Again.

Separation anxiety had taken over. Which was dumb. I wasn't a kid anymore. I was a twenty-three-year-old, employed, independent female. I shouldn't be so terrified of being left alone.

But I was. Just like when I was seventeen—the year I developed this stupid rash. I'd had the worst childhood possible, and yet, it wasn't until I was on my own that I stressed out so badly, I triggered the auto-immune disease that threatened my life every day.

Like I said, I had the worst luck possible.

My phone rang. I pulled it out of my purse, then rolled my eyes. It was Lacy, of course. My trip to Chicago had been spontaneous. Lacy knew full well I didn't do spontaneity. So, she kept calling, worried I was stressing myself out.

"I'm fine," I lied over the line and patted down my hair to hide the growing rash.

"Your location would say otherwise," she countered.

Oh, yeah, she could track my phone. When Lacy had learned that my rash could turn deadly within hours, she had insisted on keeping track of me. I had loved the idea and had agreed on the spot. She reminded me of my big brother, the one who had stayed by my side through our horrific childhood.

Until I messed up and sent him to jail.

"Did your brother say something?" she asked.

"No, he's good." Another lie. Something Lacy hated. She was adamant about being honest no matter the cost, but I hadn't found much reward in honesty.

"Isn't he due for parole soon?" she asked.

"He's got another year." Lacy would be married by then. Which meant I needed my brother back so this stupid rash wouldn't end up killing me. But he had a major problem. He was part of a gang, and that wasn't like a normal job. You couldn't hand in your two-week notice and then leave. No, you were stuck in there for life. The only way out was death.

So, I decided to free him. Which was how I ended up trapped in this dingy café. I should never have tried to be heroic. I didn't have the luck for it.

"How long are you staying in that area?" Lacy asked.

"Not too long." I needed to give up. The reason that brought me here—a certain person—could be dead for all I knew. Gang violence, in this area, claimed random lives all the time. But he once influenced my brother's gang. And I had the dumb hope that he might flex that influence for my brother.

"Sarah, I really don't like this. You're acting weird. This is about me marrying David, isn't it?"

It definitely was. But what was I supposed to say? Give up the fairytale life and come back and stay trapped with me?

No way. I ruined people, like my brother and my dead parents. But Lacy deserved this turn of good luck. I would make sure she stayed free even if it killed me.

"Like I said," I began, "my brother's birthday is coming up and I haven't seen him since we moved to New York. I didn't want him thinking I had forgotten him." My brother had been furious when I showed up to visit him in prison this morning. I had a new life, he insisted, and he didn't want me messing it up by bringing all his baggage into it.

His gang hadn't cared too much about me when I was a young, poor orphan, but now that I was connected to a woman about to marry a billionaire? Their interest would skyrocket.

"But you were supposed to be at the airport by now," Lacy countered. "You're being spontaneous again. Something's wrong."

I glowered at myself in the mirror. She knew me too well.

"Sarah." Lacy's tone had softened. "I'm not going to leave you behind like your parents and brother did. I took you with me when I got promoted, and I'll take you with me wherever I go."

"And what?" I muttered. "Do I live with you and David in his massive penthouse? Come on, Lacy. I'd end up making you two divorce."

"Stop talking like that. You'll keep the apartment we have now. And you'll come with me to the parties, and you never know... Maybe you'll meet someone—"

"No one is going to love a leper, Lacy."

"Sarah, don't call yourself that—"

"You know it's true."

"You're not a leper—"

"I'm trouble, Lacy. I always have been."

"So was I, remember? But, things can change—"

"Not for me."

"Sarah—"

"Look, I gotta go if I'm going to catch my flight." I wiggled my toes. The cream was taking effect; the pain had subsided. I could walk—gingerly, but I could walk. Time to sneak out the back.

"You're not going to make it even if you run. I'll get David to charter you a flight."

"No." It made me uncomfortable when David spent money on me. He should shower it on his fiancée, not on her useless best friend. "I'll be fine." I headed out the door, into the hallway. "I'll call you when I—"

I stopped, my eyes wide. Two big men were carrying a limp body toward the back door. And I was in their way.

I backpedaled as hard as I could into the bathroom. Which was stupid. Now I was trapped. How did I always seem to get into these messes? But if this was gang violence, they might not bother going after me. That stuff happened so often, cops no longer bothered to do anything about it.

But nope, my luck was no good. Their yells were loud. They couldn't have a witness.

"Lacy," I shot into the phone. "You're the bestest friend ever, but I'm in so much trouble. Track my—"

The door burst open, a snarling man charging forward, a gun aimed at me.

First thought: he wasn't shooting yet. Second thought: screaming would get me nowhere. Third thought: I was a girl; he was male. Pity might happen.

I flooded my eyes with tears. "Don't shoot! Please!" I raised my hands, my small purse a futile shield. "I didn't see anything! Don't hurt me!" I cowered against the wall, working my tears as hard as I could.

For the longest two seconds of my life, the thug stared at me. Then he waved the gun toward my face.

"Give me your phone!"

The phone was the only way for Lacy to track where I—or my body—ended up. But resisting would ensure death.

Lacy was yelling on the line, but I held the phone out toward the thug. He slapped my hand. Pain erupted. My hand went numb, and the phone clattered to the ground. Then an ear-splitting bang emitted from his gun. Hot, acrid smoke filled my nostrils, and I stared, wide-eyed, at my shattered phone. So much for the tracking.

He raised the gun back at me. I braced against the wall, my one fleeting thought: if I die, I wished I had perished defiantly instead of like this. But fear ruled my life, so it would rule me in death.

Except he waved his gun toward the door. "Move!"

I obeyed, my purse clutched to my chest. My feet, oddly, didn't hurt. Nor could I feel the itch. It was like I wasn't really there. My vision had gone weird, like I was peering at my life from somewhere far away. Everything was surreal, as though I was going to wake up any moment, and all of this would disappear. But the gunshot still rang in my ears, combating with the loud drums of my pumping heartbeat.

I stumbled into the hallway. The limp body was on the floor, a bag over the head, but I recognized the clothing. It was the cute guy from earlier.

"Why is she alive?" the other thug barked, guarding the limp body, but his gun swiveling to me as I came out.

"Shut it!" the first thug yelled. "Just bring Mark." He waved his gun at the back door, his eyes on me. "Out!"

My feet obeyed before my brain could catch up, and I found myself beside a beat-up car parked in the cramped alleyway. The thug opened up the trunk. It was obvious where he expected me to go. Not wanting to end up like the limp body, I climbed in. The thug stood there while the second one dragged their victim—Mark, wasn't it?—then they both hefted the body and dumped it beside me. Seconds later, the trunk slammed closed.

I lay there, not moving, not even when the car took off, heading to who-knew-where. I knew my stress levels were through the roof. I knew my disease was skyrocketing—that I possibly might die of that instead of by these thugs. And yet, the biggest question that kept running through my mind: was the cute guy next to me alive or dead?

I had been near dead bodies before but never trapped in a trunk with one. I hoped he wasn't dead. Desperately hoped for it. But if he was alive, that led to a bigger dilemma: was this Mark guy worse than the two thugs driving the car?

Gangs—assuming this was a gang thing—didn't normally kidnap opposing members unless he was a high-ranking gang guy. If that was true—and his earlier confidence and flaunting of wealth insisted it was true—then he wasn't the type of guy I wanted to be lying next to when he woke up, angry and confused. And despite the cloth over his head, the thugs hadn't bothered to tie him up. Which meant I was a convenient target to pummel for a man in a bad mood.

If my stress levels weren't already high, that thought alone would have shot them up. I scooted away—but that rubbed my back against the carpeted interior. And pain flared—along with a terrible itch.

My breath froze. My rash—it must have sprung up along my back. I needed to stop stressing out.

But how in the world was I supposed to calm down?

Breathing exercises weren't going to change the fact that I had been kidnapped and was lying next to a possibly dead or, worse, murderously angry victim. And if the rash had spread onto my face—if it was now visible—the thugs may not realize the rash wasn't contagious. Normal people freaked out seeing my rash. These guys could shoot me dead.

My hands flew to my face, checking how much the rash had grown. The itchy bumps were all over my scalp and down my back, but they had extended only a few inches over my right temple. The plethora of bangs there should hide it. For now.

I plunged a shaking hand into my purse, searching for my medicinal cream. Locating the familiar round object, I yanked it out, then popped it open, squeezing the gel onto my palm in one practiced motion. Except the pungent smell overwhelmed the cramped trunk.

Oh no. If the guy wasn't dead, this was going to wake him up. Fast.

Sure enough, the body groaned.

Sneak Peek of Saving My Billionaire Protector

Chapter Two: Mark

Twenty minutes earlier

"Pull over," I announced to my best friend.

James didn't slow down the car. "Why?"

"That girl on the sidewalk." I pointed to the window, but she was no longer in view. "She's limping. Turn around, so we can give her a ride."

"We are not turning around."

I glared at James. "I thought you were a doctor."

"I'm an orthopedist, not a paramedic, and this is a bad neighborhood. If we slow down, she'll think we're about to kidnap her, not help her."

He probably had a point, but it seemed wrong to not offer help. "We're two handsome guys, and you're wearing a suit," I countered. James had insisted on driving me even though it was going to make him late for a meeting. "We don't look like kidnappers."

"Then she might kidnap us."

I busted out laughing. "She's too small and delicate to pull off anything like that." I craned my neck to check on the girl. She was a block behind us now, but even from this distance, she looked like she was in serious pain.

"Go ahead and laugh," James continued. "But she might be a trap. People do crazy things when they think you have money."

"She has no idea we're loaded."

"Our clothes say it."

"So do hers."

He looked at me. "Really?"

"Well, not like she's super-rich, but she certainly isn't poor. Or from this neighborhood."

James slowed down, but it was to turn into a parking lot. We had arrived at our destination.

"Ignore the girl," James said. "I'm sure she knows what she's doing. You, on the other hand, don't." He waved at the dismal café that hadn't seen a heyday in decades. "This is worse than I feared. You're going to get kidnapped, and I'll get body parts sent to me along with a ransom note."

I rolled my eyes. "Now you're being dramatic. Kent will do no such thing."

"You've never met him."

"He was very polite in his emails." And effulgent with praise. He was a major fan after he'd read up on me in a magazine.

"Then why are you wearing your special tracker?"

"I like being prepared." I wasn't as paranoid as James, but Kent had acted strange. His first email, after a wall of praise, had included insisting on becoming my assistant. Which was odd since I had yet to advertise the position.

"Are you wearing your body armor, too?" James asked.

I nodded. The armor was the invention that finally launched my career. I went from a nobody to a billionaire. All my dreams came true in an instant. My worries gone.

Which might explain why I was now bored out of my mind. Hence my new interest in agreeing to potentially dangerous meetings.

"Just think." I rubbed my hands together. "This might be the start of a new career for me. Mark, the spy! Has a cool ring to it, don't you think?"

"I'll put that on your grave: Mark, the wanna-be spy who was so cool, he failed his first mission."

"How can I fail when my trusty sidekick comes in to save the day?"

"I will do no such thing."

"Yeah, right. I bet you'll miss your meeting and be around that corner, watching me the whole time."

He shook his head. "That would be stupid. They can see me from there." He pointed farther up the road. "I'll be around that corner."

I laughed and clapped him on the back. "You're the best."

"I still vehemently object to this. Nick should have asked someone else to do his dirty work."

Nick was the guy who would be monitoring my tracker. He ran the security detail that protected James' famous family and, once James told him about my odd fan, had claimed Kent wasn't a fan but a goon who worked for an evil drug lord.

James wanted me to drop all communications with the guy at once, but I was intrigued. Why was a drug lord targeting me? Yeah, I was slightly famous, but if this drug lord was looking for someone to ransom, I was the wrong guy. I had no family, and James wouldn't drop a dime for me.

So, I kept up the farce, emailing back and forth, trying to get more information, but Kent stuck to his story really well—to the point where I wasn't sure Nick was right anymore. Yeah, Kent was a bit strange, but he seemed a lot like me when I was a clueless young kid, desperate to make my mark on the world.

Then I mentioned I'd be visiting his hometown, Chicago. He immediately begged me to visit him—but with a particular condition. He was in trouble and needed help. As in thousands-of-dollars help. The kind of request I'd imagine a thug asking a rich guy. I didn't want to believe it—he'd been so nice—but I didn't want to be stupid, either. So, I contacted Nick, and a plan was hatched.

If Kent was harmless, I'd be out in ten minutes, glad to have helped someone in need. But if Kent was anything like Nick claimed, well, that was why I had the tracker, tainted money, and body armor.

I opened the car door. "Wish me luck."

"I wish you brains," James said. "You need that more than luck."

I laughed. "I'll take both, then." I stepped out, then waved as James pulled back into the street, heading for his corner. I looked at the café but didn't go in.

Despite everything, that limping girl still bothered me.

I stepped to the sidewalk. She was the only other person in sight, a petite girl with long black hair that covered most of her face as if she didn't want the world to see her. She also wore a baggy turtleneck and loose jeans despite the warm day. At her slow pace, she'd reach me in about ten minutes.

Hmmm, without a car, I couldn't really help. Unless she would be okay with me carrying her in my arms. That could be fun, but I doubted she'd be fine with it.

I dithered for another moment. I hated seeing someone in pain, but James was right. I couldn't help her.

Shooting her one last look, I sighed and entered the café.

No one was inside. Not even a bartender. I sank onto one of the stools at the counter and drummed my fingers. It was five minutes before someone finally emerged from the kitchen and seemed shocked to find me. The waiter scurried to my side, and I ordered two drinks for myself and Kent as well as two glasses of water. The AC in this place must have died because it was too hot in here.

I resumed my drumming as the server disappeared into the kitchen. Kent was late. James wasn't going to appreciate that. I wasn't appreciating it, either.

The door finally swung open. I stood up to greet Kent but found the girl instead. Woah, not a girl. A woman. And a pretty one despite her trying to cover herself up with all that black hair.

As if she could hear my thoughts, she immediately patted down her hair like that could somehow make her invisible.

"Hi," I said, but the server showed up at that moment, meaning I had to focus on paying for my drinks instead of the pretty woman.

"Where's the bathroom?" she asked the server.

He pointed to a soiled door at the back of the café, then retreated into his kitchen again. It was like the guy had no desire to have customers.

She moved forward in an obvious attempt to keep as much distance between herself and me as possible, but she also winced with each step.

I leaned against the counter. "You don't need to avoid me. You can take the shorter route." I indicated for her to pass close by me.

She ignored my offer and maintained the wide berth between us. But it was killing me watching her mince forward as if she stepped on shards of glass. I wished I could pick her up. I'd cover the ground in seconds while it took her minutes. But I had a feeling she'd start screaming if I moved an inch toward her. If only there was a way to show I meant no harm...

"Want a drink?" I waved a hand at the glasses beside me. With her turtleneck and long sleeves, along with the lack of AC, she had to be burning up. "I'll put it at the end of the counter so you don't have to come near me." I slid one of the glasses of water to the edge, then returned to my stool.

She had stopped the instant I had moved, her eyes on me like the feral cat I had once found trapped under my gramps' porch. Not a great comparison since that cat never warmed up to me. I still had scars on my hands and arms from all its scratches.

"I'm just trying to be helpful," I said. The cat never understood that concept, but hopefully, this girl would.

She shook her head. "I do not need any help."

"You sure? You look like you're in pain."

The glare on her face told me she'd rather die of that pain than accept any help from me.

"All right." I turned toward the counter and let her wince her way to the back door, my offered drink ignored. So much for trying to be nice.

I retrieved the drink, then sat and waited for Kent. He showed up seven minutes later, a normal-looking guy just like in his photo. But I hadn't expected his buddy—or the guns.

James was going to rub this in for years, wasn't he?

One kidnap later...

My head ached. And something foul penetrated the air. Along with something itchy and coarse rubbing my face.

What was going on?

Oh, yeah. Kent. And that buddy of his. With guns raised, they had demanded the money, but once I produced it, that buddy of his whacked me good.

I checked my right ankle at once, rubbing my left foot against it. The bracelet was still there. Good. Nick should be sending in his team, and then I was out of here.

Unless Nick wanted to see where they were going to take me. The whole point of this charade was to catch the evil drug lord, and I could see Nick waiting to see if that was where I ended up.

I should have listened to James.

At least I still had my body armor on me. The goons hadn't bothered to tear that off. Then again, it was my less bulky version, like a tight undershirt, so they probably had no idea what it was. Good for me. But, it was designed against knives, not bullets.

First, I had to figure out what was covering my face. Shaking my head back and forth, I deduced the itchy thing was a bag that obviously hadn't been cleaned in a while. Thankfully, Kent hadn't bothered to tie me up, so I ripped the bag off at once, then found blackness staring at me. And that foul smell—it was more profound outside of the bag. Where had Kent dumped me?

The hum filling my ears was familiar. I must be in a car. And judging by the darkness, I was in the trunk. A small part of me thought that was pretty cool, but the other part was no longer keen on being a spy. Being kidnapped wasn't anywhere as cool as the movies made it out to be.

I checked my pockets, hoping Kent had been stupid enough to leave my phone alone. Nope, he hadn't been stupid. My wallet was gone, too, along with the tainted money. And what was that pungent odor stinking up this trunk?

Stretching my hands out, my right one hit the solid edge of the trunk. My left, however, touched something squishy and warm. A body.

I snatched my hand back at once. Was it dead? Was that what was causing the smell? No, the smell was too sharp. It reminded me of a doctor's office, not a coroner's. And a dead body would be stiff and cold like my grandpa's. But that didn't answer the bigger question: where did Kent get the second body?

Since it was farther inside the trunk than me, it had been put in first. Which meant Kent could have picked it up any time before me. Great. Just what I needed. Kent wasn't only a lying backstabber but apparently a serial kidnapper, too.

"Hey," I barked in the direction of the body. "You alive?"

"Please don't hurt me."

I froze. That was a girl's voice.

"You okay?"

"Please don't hurt me." She sounded terrified. Well, I couldn't blame her. If I wasn't so furious, I'd be in the same boat.

"How do you know Kent?" I asked.

"I don't know anything. I don't want to know anything. Please don't tell me anything."

Well, she certainly was decisive. But at least she wasn't screaming like a lunatic.

"You may not want to know anything, but I do," I said. "Why are you in here? Do you know?"

"I saw them dragging you out."

Oh, ouch. She was an innocent bystander now roped into my mess. Still, she had more information than me.

"Out the front door?" I asked.

"Out the back."

Something wiggled at the back of my mind. Someone else had gone into the back. And she wouldn't have been able to run away...

"Are you the girl who went to the bathroom?"

There was a slight pause. "Yes."

I mentally cursed. It may be old-fashioned, but Gramps had insisted a gentleman never cursed in the presence of a lady. But I was livid at myself. All I wanted to do was help, but now she might end up dead because of me.

"Sorry," I said out loud.

She made no reply. I couldn't blame her. My apology was pretty useless.

"Did they hurt you?" I asked.

"No."

"Good." At least Kent and his buddy had some morals. "What's your name?"

She was silent. The image of that suspicious feral cat came to my mind.

"I'm Mark," I offered. "I—"

The car abruptly stopped. It had been doing that several times, no doubt for stoplights, but this time, the engine turned off as well. We must have arrived at our destination.

I debated putting the bag back on my head—it might give me the element of surprise if they didn't know I was conscious. But then, they had guns and I didn't. Yeah, I had body armor, but it wouldn't save me from a barrage of bullets. And I had no protection against a headshot. Nor was I cool enough to take on two armed men with my bare hands. Though now that a girl was involved, I wished I had followed James' advice and taken a self-defense class before meeting Kent.

Leaving the bag off, I leveled my best glare at Kent when he opened the trunk. He avoided my gaze. Either I had a more impressive glare than I thought or he wasn't too proud of the backstabbing.

"Get out," his buddy barked.

I complied and found myself at a lonely dock, a dejected, small speedboat tied up, ready for boarding. Uh oh, I hadn't considered they might haul me over water. Nick hadn't told me if his tracker used satellites. If it only used cell phone towers, the signal could drop, and Nick might not find me. I scanned the dock, hoping to see Nick's team pop out, but instead, a tall, thin man—his face covered with a bandanna—emerged from the boat, a gun in his hands.

He surveyed me like I was days-old meat at the market, but then his eyes shot to the girl as she climbed out.

"Why the chick?" the new guy demanded, flicking his chin toward her.

"She saw us," Kent confessed.

"Then why ain't she dead?"

"She got nice clothes," Kent continued. "Figured we could get a ransom."

Her eyes widened at his statement.

The new guy sneered at the girl. "You important? You got anybody rich?"

That was a dumb question. It didn't matter what the truth was, the obvious answer was yes if she wanted to live.

But she just stared at the new guy for a long moment as if racking her brain for anyone who might qualify. Then she shook her head.

The guy raised his gun.

I only had one thought: she was not dying on my account.

"She's important to me." I stepped between her and the gun. "My people will pay for the both of us."

The new guy eyed me. I matched his gaze, daring him to doubt me. I had no idea what Kent had told these buddies of his, but for them to bother to do this whole kidnapping thing, they had to think money was going to come from somewhere.

He finally shrugged. "Toss 'em both."

Kent nodded, then waved his gun at me and the girl. I indicated for the girl to go first. She did, albeit slowly. Her feet must still hurt. What did she do to them?

As she passed the new guy, however, he swiped the purse out of her hands. I instinctively took a step forward, but he shot me a warning growl. Since I knew I could do nothing, I backed down and glowered as he rifled through the purse. He soon found a wallet. He ignored the credit cards and removed a small amount of cash. Then he tossed the purse into the water. The girl gasped, alarmed eyes on the purse as it sank, but she made no other protest.

"Move!" Kent barked as if we were cattle. I shot him a glare but followed the girl as she got onto the small boat. It swayed as all five of us clambered on board, then the new guy moved to the back end and pulled up a compartment door. The inside was obviously not designed for two people. We would have to lie down, curled up against each other.

Awkward.

I let the girl drop in first. To my surprise, she didn't lie down but tucked her petite self against the far wall lengthwise, her back against one wall, knees up to her chest, and her feet against the other side.

Okay, not so awkward.

I lowered my large frame into the tiny space left over, sitting down, then bent my body over my knees and barely avoided the lid slamming onto my head. It was a most unpleasant position to be in. I hoped the final destination wasn't far, or this was going to be one miserable ride. Worse, being locked up in here with no access to the sky meant that Nick's tracker, if it had GPS capability, wouldn't work anyway.

The engine soon revved up, and the boat lurched forward.

"Thank you," the girl said. The engine noise was loud in this cramped space, but since her face was a few inches from mine, I heard her fine. "You didn't have to save me like that," she continued.

"Yeah, I did." I turned my head to see if I could see her face, but it was too dark to catch anything. "It's my fault you're in this. The least I can do is make sure you don't die. But you should have lied. Being dishonest and alive is better than honest and dead."

She was quiet for a moment. "Does that mean you lied? That there isn't anyone who's going to pay the ransom for me?"

Smart girl. "If it makes you feel any better, no one's going to pay for me either."

"That does not make me feel better." She took a deep breath, blew it out slowly, then repeated the process. I recognized that move. My Nana used to do that when she was trying not to freak out.

"You're going to be okay," I said.

"You don't even know if you're going to be okay."

Wow, she had a sharp tongue. And she obviously was not into cheap platitudes. "When I said no one was going to pay for me, that didn't mean no one's coming. My friends are the type who would prefer finding thugs instead of paying them. And, when my friends find me—and they will find me—I'll be taking you with me. That, I swear."

She was silent for several seconds. "How long do you think it will take for your friends to find you?"

I had no idea but I wasn't going to confess that. "Twenty-four hours tops."

Her breathing quickened. "I might be dead before then. My medicine; it's all gone."

That didn't sound good. "What type of medicine?"

"I'm sorry, but can we talk about something else? Please?" Panic tinged her tone.

I had no desire to divert from the ominous topic of her medicine, but neither did I want her dissolving into a panic attack. "Could I ask what's wrong with your feet?"

"I need something that has not happened today." Her breath was coming faster. "Like four days ago. That was a good day. A really good day." She was rambling. "No surprises. No stress. Everything went according to plan. I passed my swimming test. I can officially swim. Except now I'm on a boat. In water. To die." She sucked in her breath as if about to scream.

"How long have you been swimming?" I shot out.

She exhaled her sharp intake in a controlled manner. "I, uh, started taking lessons with a good friend of mine some months ago. She was determined to learn how to swim, and she dragged me along. Ironic, right?"

"Lucky, I'd say. I bet you swim better than me."

"You don't know how to swim?"

"I know enough to stay afloat, but if I had to race, I wouldn't be the winner."

"That's about where I'm at, too." She repeated her breathing exercise. In and out. In and out.

Hmm, I knew a trick that might take her mind off things. "You have family?"

There was a sharp intake of breath again.

Oops, maybe not. "Bad topic?"

"I...have a brother. You?"

"I hear I got sisters and brothers, but I've never met them."

There was a pause. I grinned. That response shocked people every time.

"I'm sorry, say that again?" she asked.

"My mom had me too young, then took off when I was one or two. Last I heard, she had married a rich fellow in California and has a score of kids now."

"She never tried to come and see you?"

"Her parents ended up raising me; Gramps and my mom, they never got along. I believe he told her to never come back, so she didn't."

"Oh, I'm sorry."

"Nah, it's not a big deal. My grandparents were good to me. A little slow, but good. Gramps was an inventor. Or at least, he liked to believe he was one. He never succeeded in inventing anything useful, but he sure knew how to blow up his garage. It was cool. You should have seen it."

I had no idea why I said that. Women didn't like explosions. They liked money and shopping and shoes, not the crazy antics of a slightly deranged old fool.

But to my surprise, she chuckled. "Did you help him in those endeavors?"

"Nah," I said. "He only let me blow up little stuff."

That produced another chuckle. "What were the things he tried to invent?"

I launched into some of his sillier ideas, hoping to get more chuckles out of her. But she didn't chuckle. She laughed. In all the right spots. And then kept asking for more. I couldn't believe it. No girl had ever shown interest in my Gramps's antics before.

Well, that wasn't entirely true. After the money came rolling in, girls had shown abundant interest—as long as expensive gifts came with it. I'd gone along with the game at first. Women having an interest in me was a new thing, and I didn't care what the price was. But James insisted it would get old.

And it did.

Two years later, their fake laughs and timed giggles simply grated on my nerves. Now, I understood why James refused to enter the dating game. I was starting to lean that way myself.

But this girl had no reason to fake interest. Then again, she was probably desperate to focus on something other than the fact that she was kidnapped.

No, she had too sharp of a tongue. Like the feral cat, if she didn't like something, I'd know it.

I suddenly wished I had met her at a gala. I would have asked her out on the spot. Anyone who could enjoy the stories of Gramps was a person worthy of getting to know better. But I couldn't say a thing right now. James might tease that I hit on any girl that moved, but I did have some standards.

And a gentleman did not flirt with a girl who was kidnapped.

Especially when I was the reason she was in this mess. I bet the only thing she wanted from me was to stay as far away from her as possible.

Now I really hated being kidnapped.

Buy SAVING MY BILLIONAIRE PROTECTOR now!

Other Books by Leena D'Wynter

Smitten Billionaires Series

#1 Trusting My Billionaire Boss (Lacy and David)
#2 Saving My Billionaire Protector (Sarah and Mark)
#3 Believing My Billionaire Surgeon (Celeste and James)
#4 Fake-Dating My Billionaire Enemy (Samantha and Henry)
#5 Mending My Billionaire Rockstar (Stacy and Ace)

Made in United States
North Haven, CT
29 August 2023